Polish Herbs,
Flowers &
Folk Medicine

Also by Sophie Hodorowicz Knab:

Polish Customs, Traditions & Folklore

Polish
Herbs, Flowers &
Folk Medicine

Sophie Hodorowicz Knab

Illustrations by Mary Anne Knab

HIPPOCRENE BOOKS
New York, NY

For information, address:
HIPPOCRENE BOOKS, INC.
171 Madison Avenue
New York, NY 10016

Library of Congress Cataloging-in Publication Data
Knab, Sophie Hodorowicz.
  Polish herbs, flowers & folk medicine / Sophie Hodorowicz Knab :
illustrations by Mary Anne Knab.
              p.   cm.
  Includes bibliographical references (p.   ) and index.
  ISBN 0-7818-0319-5
  1. Herbs.   2. Herb gardening.   3. Herbs--Therapeutic use.
4. Flowers.   5. Flower gardening.   6. Plants, Useful.   7. Herb
gardens--Poland--History.   I. Title.
SB351.H5K635   1995
581.6'1'09438--dc20   95-22712
                                                        CIP

Printed in the United States of America.

Dedicated to my husband,
Edward Joseph Knab

Contents

GDAŃSK

WARMIA

POMERANIA

• SZCZECIN

BAIŁYSTOK •

BYDGOSZCZ
•

BISKUPIN
•

WISŁA

PODLASIE

• POZNAŃ

MAZOVIA

BUG

GREAT POLAND

• WARSAW

ŁOWICZ
•

POLAND

ODRA

• LUBLIN

SILESIA

• WROCŁAW

• OPOLE

SAN

LITTLE

• TARNOBRZEG

WISŁA

POLAND

RZESZÓW
•

• KRAKÓW

• ZAKOPANE

Acknowledgments

I would like to thank the following individuals for their help with this book:

First thanks must go to Rev. Czesław Krysa, friend and Polish folklore enthusiast *extraordinaire*, whose kind and generous heart helped me obtain copies of the Polish periodicals that contained so much of the material used in this book. Without them this book truly would not have been possible;

To Michael Miecznikowski who gave me my very first opportunity to put on a display of Polish herbs for the public and his sister-in-law Jo Anne Miecznikowski who was willing to do it with me—and what a success it was!

To the wonderful librarians and staff at Niagara County Community College who are always there for me whatever my inquiry—Kathleen Greenfield, Fran Angelleti, Gail Staines, Linda Herman, Beth Hodgeson, Nancy Verstreate, Jeanne Tuohey, Catherine Gibbs, Lillian Passanese and Karen Ferington. You're the best;

To Judy Krauza, who never tires of preserving and promoting Polish culture and always seems to find time to be supportive of her friends;

To Dr. and Mrs. Tadeusz Pyzikiewicz for their very generous loan of Polish gardening books and magazines from their private collection;

To my brothers Michael, Andrew and Matthew Hodorowicz and their families for their constant help and interest; a special thank you to my nephew Luke Hodorowicz for the computer consultations;

POLISH HERBS, FLOWERS & FOLK MEDICINE

To my sister-in-law Mary Anne Knab for her commitment and enthusiasm in working with me on my projects and capturing the Polish garden in drawings;

To Paula Redes and Jacek Galazka at Hippocrene Books for their unstinting support and editorial skills that make writing so much easier.

In Poland I would like to thank Krystyna Bartosik of the Warsaw Ethnographic Museum who so graciously helped me locate materials while visiting there; Grażyna Czerwiński, curator at the Museum in Sierpc who helped me document the herbs and perennials in cottage gardens and Henryka Lus of Łowicz for creating the paper cut-out used for the cover of this book;

Lastly, an enormous thank you to all the libraries and librarians throughout North America who continue to keep and safeguard their Polish book collections so that works can be accessed and utilized. It is these collections that make my books possible;

To all of you, *Bóg zapłać*.

Introduction

In this book I return to the material that led me to write *Polish Customs, Traditions and Folklore*. I realized that I wanted to complete the work that I had begun so many years ago in graduate school and document the history and use of herbs and folk medicine in Poland as well as try to understand how the people of Poland viewed the issues of health and illness.

My interest in herbs, however, started extending beyond the use of plants in folk medicine and into gardening itself. I began to wonder about the gardens of Poland: What types of gardens were popular in Poland? Did they have knot gardens? If they did, what kinds of herbs and flowers were grown in them? What flowers were typical in a cottage garden? What plants were used to dye wools and linens?

I offer you the end result of my findings. Besides learning about the various herbs used in health, illness and healing, I discovered a heritage that will continuously influence my gardening from this moment on. It is not just having a garden design to copy, although I found that to be extremely exciting, but it's knowing something about the herbs and flowers that I'm planting or see growing along the roadside or in a field. They've become a link with the most ancient of my ancestors. While the Polish people no longer strew calamus on their floors during high holidays, or stuff their mattresses with the leaves of larkspur to keep the insects away or hang bunches of herbs to perfume a room, it's a really nice feeling to know that they once did.

All suggestions within this book are made without guarantee on the part of the author or Hippocrene Books, Inc.

The information in this book is chiefly for reference and education. It is not intended as a substitute for the advice of a physician. The reader should be aware that any plant substance, whether used as food or medicine, internally or externally, may cause an allergic reaction.

CHAPTER I

Flowers and Herbs in
Everyday Polish Life

In 1933, Polish archeologists unearthed the remains of an ancient settlement that provided much information about Poland's early development. It was called Biskupin and is located in the Bydgoszcz province. Careful reconstruction dated the civilization back to 550-400 B.C. From these discoveries, it became clear that farming and raising cattle were the chief occupations of the inhabitants. They grew wheat, barley, rye and beans. The archeologists determined that these early peoples of Poland used herbs not only to flavor foods but also as medication. Twenty different herbs were identified at the site. Among those listed were mullein, asarum, burdock, wormwood, coltsfoot, mallow and tansey. There was also no doubt that these early Slavs had had cults revering plants, animals and trees and attributed great magic, strength and power to them. Trees were worshipped as divine. The forests were considered the dwelling place of the gods. Worshipers laid offerings before the trees and used their branches in rituals throughout the changing cycle of the seasons.

In 966, Polish King Mieszko accepted Christianity for the people of his lands. The old pagan practices of worshiping plants and trees were not eradicated but rather became intermingled with the new religion and persisted throughout the centuries. Even as late as the 16th century, the authorities were still attempting to put a stop to the custom of "stripping the forest to celebrate the onset of spring" without much success.

In the late 1800's, when folklore scholars were documenting the folk life of the peasants, they found that very ancient practices tied to primitive beliefs about plants and trees, were still abundantly evident. Every facet of life—from the day-to-day routine, to family and community celebrations, to the designs on clothing, furniture and common household utensils—reflected a close communion with plants and plant life.

Early spring saw groups of young girls parading through their villages with a budding young tree called a *maik* or *gaik* as a symbol of the emergence of new life: continuing the ancient cycle of birth, death, and rebirth. On Palm Sunday, churchgoers cut branches of birch, raspberry, or any nearby tree. They then placed them in water in a warm room to accelerate the budding process. In the northern Kurpie region, where vast tracts of forests covered the countryside, the palms for Palm Sunday were made of long wooden poles, covered with club moss, heather, willow and billberry. Flowers were made from the white center of the bullrush plant and attached along the length of the pole. An evergreen branch was fastened at the top.

Spring was the time for many other customs involving forest greenery. One of the first traditions of the season was called *dyngus*. Young men either doused young unmarried girls with water or playfully hit them with branches of early blossoming pussy willows or the evergreen branches of juniper or birch. There were May Day celebrations with the erection of May poles decorated with flowers and boughs of greenery while the rest of the community sang and danced around its perimeter. Men took their cattle out to the fields for the first time, touching them with a green branch and weaving wreathes made of flowers and herbs around their necks and horns. The green holidays (Pentecost, Whitsuntide) saw doors and windowsills decorated with branches of birch, pine and spruce. Sweet flag was strewn on the floors and entrances to the house.

The feast of Corpus Christi, the Catholic Church's commemoration of the Holy Eucharist, was also celebrated with a great display of plants. On this day, four different altars were erected at various points within a town or village. Each altar was decorated with an abundance of greenery, birch branches in particular. Wreaths as small as the palm of a hand, made from various herbs and flowers, were blessed in church by the priest. In the Podlasie area, which runs along the Narew River, people wove nine small wreaths, each made from a different herb:

thyme, hazelwort, stonecrop, lady's mantle, sundew, mint, rue, daisy and periwinkle. The wreaths were hung on the monstrance where they stayed for the week following Corpus Christi. In some parts of Poland the herbs and flowers were formed into a wreath and attached to strips of paper on which exerpts from the gospels were written. When the eight day celebration of Corpus Christi was over, the wreaths were taken home and hung on the wall above holy pictures. They, too, served in various capacities in the home. They were placed under the foundation of a newly-built house to ward off evil spirits and protect the home from natural and manmade disasters. Some of the herbs from the wreaths were crumbled and burnt as a form of incense for those suffering from dropsy, an early term for edema. The smoke from thyme and stonecrop was believed capable of dispersing hail clouds and lightning, thereby saving grain crops from destruction.

The summer solstice, later called St. John's Eve, was another day richly laden with herbal traditions in Poland. On this night, certain plants had the power of both creating happiness and warding off evil spirits.

No other plant played as important a role on this night as mugwort, so much so that the midsummer bonfires were also called mugwort fires. A garland of the herb thrown on a midsummer fire would render the thrower safe from all ill-fortune for the next twelve months. If one held up a garland and peered through it at the bonfire, it would prevent headaches and smarting eyes. It also had the power to repel witches. In the Śląsk region, the midsummer wreath was made of nine different herbs: marjoram, madder, thyme, lovage, savory, basil, fennel, angelica and hyssop. Girls would throw the wreath on the fire calling loudly "Let go and burn, everything that gives me pain!"

Numerous other herbs were credited with having the power to repel witches and evils on this night. St. John's wort was hung above the doors of houses and barns. Madness could be cured by drinking a potion made from it. Vervain, along with burdock, hazel and wormwood was hung above the entrances of many Polish cottages as protection against evil forces.

Herbs gathered on the night of the summer solstice were thought to possess more than their usual curing powers. Aged men, women and children headed for the fields and woods in search of clover, chamomile and coltsfoot. If gathered before sunset, these herbs were thought to be especially useful for such illnesses as rheumatism, arthritis and lung problems.

The search for the male fern flower was of special importance on this night. It was believed that somewhere in a wild place the barren male fern bloomed a flower at midnight. The flower, if found, was said to give the owner the power to see beneath the earth where secret treasures lay hidden. Whosoever found it would be sure to experience good fortune. This magical flower, however, was very small, difficult to see and unlikely to be discovered because it was guarded by the devil himself.

One of the most important vestiges preserved from the time when the ancient people of Poland gathered and worshiped greenery—and still actively practiced today in rural areas—is the present day Feast of Our Lady of the Herbs.

The festival occurs on August 15th, when the earth is at its most giving; the forests are heavy with berries and nuts; the fields are thick with ripened grains gently swaying in the breeze; the food crops are at full maturity and ready to be harvested. In ancient times, the people that inhabited Poland rejoiced in the magic of the earth yielding such bounty, and gave homage to the gods. They brought these first fruits from the forests and fields to their altars in celebration and offered it up to those they thought responsible for the gifts. Societal influences and the passage of time have greatly changed the celebration's name and focus, however, the original character has remained intact.

For this day, each village housewife went out and gathered her favorite herbs and flowers along with branches of fruit and nut trees to form a large bouquet. Both garden herbs and flowers, as well as those growing in the wild, were collected. This included field poppy, mugwort, tansy, henbane and mullein from the fields. She would cut lily, sage, thyme, dill, and lemon balm from her garden as well as branches of fir, hazel or juniper from the forests. Because the holiday fell when the grain harvest was ripe, it was also customary to take a few spikes of the various grains of millet, barley, rye and wheat. Having gathered all that she wanted, the housewife, along with the other women of the village, would bring her bouquet to church where the priest would say Mass and bless all the bouquets.

The newly blessed flowers and herbs were carefully taken home and used in a variety of important ways. Most often the entire bouquet was woven into a single wreath while the herbs and flowers were still fresh and pliable and hung near or over a holy picture to dry. The housewife would then use the dried material as she needed it. For instance, she would crumble some of the blessed and dried flowers into a bag of seed when her husband was going out to the field to sow for the first time in spring. She did this in the hope that the sowing would be a successful one and yield a handsome harvest. If a cow went dry, she would burn some of the herbs as an incense to get the cow producing milk again.

Sometimes the flowers and herbs were separated and dried according to their future purpose. Some of the herbs were tied to a string and hung from a nail under the eaves of the house to protect it from lightning, fire, communicable diseases and other major disasters. A portion of the herbs would be dried and stored safely away in cloth bags for future needs, especially medicinal ones.

The majority of people in Poland lived in small, rural villages far removed from large cities with practicing physicians. Each person depended on his/her own knowledge and comprehension of health and illness to treat individual aches and pains. The traditional Polish housewife believed that the healing properties of all the plants and herbs she collected were more effective when blessed. Therefore, she collected and stored her plants carefully and used them to make teas, salves and poultices—both for humans and livestock.

Flowers have always had a language of their own and in Polish customs and traditions this is especially so. Wreathes made of flowers and greenery became headdresses worn strictly by young unmarried girls as a symbol of their maidenly virtue. They wore them to church and on all special occasions to differentiate them from the married women (wearing scarves or caps). In this manner, men visiting a village could

Wedding Branch

immediately discern the single females from the married women. However, girls who had a child out of wedlock were forbidden from wearing wreathes made of flowers; they were no longer considered pure.

Rue growing in a cottage garden was a sign that a marriageable daughter lived within and was preparing for her wedding day. Rosemary and myrtle growing on a windowsill was another unspoken sign that someone was waiting to be married.

Herbs and flowers played a tremendously large role in wedding traditions. The night before her wedding day, the young maiden would go to her garden to cut down the rue she had so carefully planted for this important night. She would gather her chosen bridesmaids around her and amidst much singing weave a wreath of rue to wear to church the next day.

In some parts of Poland, the preferred plant for the bride was myrtle or rosemary decorated with flowers and ribbons. The groom and groomsmen adorned their hats with peacock feathers or a flowery twig tucked into the bands. An important component of wedding celebrations was the *rózga weselna*—the wedding rod or wedding branch. This was most often an evergreen branch of pine, juniper or spruce that had at least two side branches as well as a central one. It was prepared by the bridesmaids for the bride, decorating it with ribbons, artificial flowers, apples and nuts. On it, the groom attached his wedding gift to his wife and it was solemnly given to her during a special part of the wedding ceremony.

In birth and in death, plants also figured strongly. Yarrow was used to regulate menstruation. Mugwort was used to increase fertility. Southernwood supposedly helped prevent miscarriages. During the time of birthing, St. John's wort was hung in the window to scare away evil spirits. Branches of willow in the form of a cross were also placed in the home to scatter any evil spirits. The herbs blessed on Corpus Christi which contained lemon balm, southernwood, and cornflower were used to protect both mother and child. After delivery, the new mother would receive a strengthening cup of chamomile or lemon balm tea. Mistletoe was tucked into the cradle to give the infant pleasant dreams and southernwood and mugwort, tucked under the infant's shirt, protected it against the evil eye. Mugwort, lovage and thyme, as well as the leaves of the hazel tree, were used in the baby's first bath.

In very tiny villages, death was announced to the community by throwing periwinkle on the doorstep of a house and calling out the name of the person that had passed away. Each house was expected to move the herb along to the next until it arrived back to the house of the deceased. Juniper berries were used to incense the dead body. A pillow for the deceased was made of wood shavings to which wormwood, tansy, southernwood, mugwort or thyme were added. Mugwort and wormwood were tucked around the body. Sometimes a wreath made from a fir tree was placed under the head of the deceased. Even the graveyard told its tale through flowers and plants. If the family could not afford to erect a cross, a favorite flower or herb once enjoyed by the deceased was used to mark the grave. Boxthorn was planted on the graves of those who were murdered.

Flowers in Folk Art

History has shown that agriculture continued to be Poland's chief economic base well into the 20th century. For over two thousand years the majority of the population lived and worked on the land as nomadic tribes, serfs, peasants and tenant farmers. The fertile lands provided wheat, oats and rye as nourishment for man and animal. The land yielded wild herbs for seasoning, plants for dyeing yarns, flowers for adorning altars, roots and leaves for healing and saplings for brooms, fences and basket work. The land also became the source of inspiration for man's creativity.

Perhaps the painting or carving of plant life on tools and weapons originated when seeking the help of the supernatural or when trying to imitate the forms and intrinsic beauty of nature. Perhaps it was an attempt to give expression to thoughts, feelings and the need to beautify the surrounding environment. Whatever the reasoning, ever since early

Base of Distaff of Spinning Wheel carved with hearts, birds and plants.

21

Cut paper or *wycinanki*, with roosters, birds and deer.

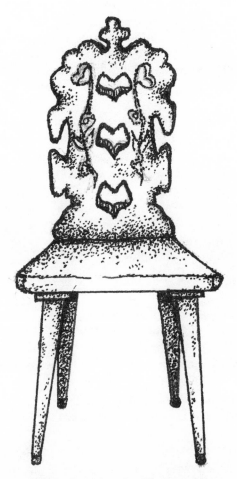

Chair Decorated with Poppies

man began making tools, clothes, and stools, he has attempted to make them beautiful. Living, working and dying in close proximity to the land, the men and women of Poland drew their decorative motifs from that which they knew best—the herbs, flowers and trees of the field and forest.

In the 19th century, with the advent of the chimney in peasant cottages, there began numerous attempts to make the interior look attractive. The walls—no longer in danger of being blackened by the smoke that had constantly hung within the house—began to be whitewashed. On these newly whitened walls, the peasant women began to beautify their homes. Painting freehand or with primitive templates made from potatoes, the women dipped liberally into their own dyepots and painted fantastic flower designs on walls, ceilings and furniture. Filled with color and imagination, their homes were transformed into bowers of greenery complete with roses, dahlias, bluebells and birds sitting atop twigs. Not limiting themselves to interior walls, they expanded their canvases to their homes' exterior and the surrounding objects. Barn doors, dog houses and water wells mirrored the flowers growing in the garden, the fields and the riverbanks.

Other peasant women beautified their homes by hanging pictures of the saints on the walls and decorating these portraits with wreathes or bouquets of artificial flowers that they had made from dyed wood shavings or colored tissue paper, if they were fortunate enough to come by it.

In some parts of Poland, such as the Łowicz and the Kurpie region, a folk art form called *wycinanki* dominated as an interior decoration. Using colored paper and sheepshears, both men and women brought the life that abounded in the meadows and forest into their homes. Roosters, birds, and deer motifs were among the favorite shapes and themes that emerged from the carefully folded and cut paper, but the flower motif predominated. There were single blossoms, whole bouquets, as well as numerous stylized versions of the tree-of-life. All of these were pasted on whitewashed walls, usually after the seasonal housecleaning, in the early spring.

Leluja-stylized "Tree of Life"

Flower motif was popular cut-paper motif.

FLOWERS AND HERBS IN EVERYDAY POLISH LIFE

Besides the walls, floors received special attention during springtime through the use of sandpainting. Even after chimnneys became common, the floors of peasant cottages were still made from hard-packed earth. Using fine white sand, the housewife would "write" on the dark, black floor in preparation for Sunday, but especially for the time of the Green Holidays. She would pour the sand from the edge of a closed fist or a pot with a small hole in it. While some of the designs consisted of circles, geometric shapes, roosters and people, the predominant motifs used by the women were of stylized flowers. This custom was tied very closely to central Poland, especially on the left bank of the Wisła such as Opoczno, Rawa, Kielce, Łowicz and Kujawy. It was still being drawn by women in these regions as late as 1900.

From the moment people began putting down wooden floors inside their homes, sandpainting was relegated to the outside. On a Saturday, or the day before a holiday, the yard in front of the house was swept clean and decorated with sand. Sometimes the housewives also sprinkled calamus and other herbs around the doorstep.

The common everyday objects found within the home did not escape decoration. Poland was a country of vast plains but it also contained tremendous tracts of forests. Wood was used to make practically all utensils for household and domestic use. One of the customs commonly observed in Poland was that of presenting young girls with decorated objects connected with domestic work. Carved spoons or spoon racks, wooden ladles, gingerbread molds, butter molds and shuttles were elaborately carved by young men intent on courtship. Spindles and distaffs for spinning were especially popular gifts. The most richly ornamented part of the distaff was the base. In addition to carving, there was also inlaid work and painting. The ornamentation included birds, geometrical patterns, plants, motifs of twigs and leaves, flowers and trees. When offered to a young woman, these objects became unspoken symbols of her suitor's feelings and intentions. He poured considerable thought, skill, effort and emotion into various household items so as to best reflect the depth of his ardor. When the girls met at one another's cottages to spend the long winter evening spinning their wool or flax, it not only helped to decrease the boredom

Water well painted with peacocks, wheat and flowers.

Dowry Chest Painted with Flowers

and monotony of winter, but also provided the girls with an opportunity to show off the tokens of affection they had received from their intendeds.

The dower or trousseau chests were another household item which received a great deal of attention. According to Polish tradition, the girl of the house filled it with pillows and sheets made on the loom to take to her future home. They also served as wardrobes in which to keep Sunday-best clothes and jewelry. The chests were beautifully painted with bouquets of flowers (the classic Polish symbol of maidenly virtue), tied with a ribbon or simply set into a pot against a red, brown, yellow or green background. Besides beautifying their homes and the objects within it, the peasant men and women of Poland also sought to beautify themselves. It is almost impossible to go into detail in this brief chapter on a subject of such scope, but it warrants mentioning that through studying embroidery patterns and motifs in folk dress, one can learn the flowers that dominated a particular region. For instance, the *górale*, the people living in the Tatra mountain region, used flowers indigenous to the area. Lilium martagon, carline thistle and edelweiss prevailed on women's bodices and vests. In Kujawy, the predominant flower was the clover from the meadows. A careful study of old aprons in the Kujawy

Butter Mold

region reveals borders of grapevine, cornflower and aster. The most frequently used motif, however, was the rose. From its unique style, it could be recognized amongst all other embroidered rose styles as the Kujawy rose. In the Kaszuby region, in the north of Poland, the tulip and hundreds of stylized versions of it reigns supreme in practically all manner of embroidery and needlework.

In the final analysis—whatever the aspect of life, whatever the region of Poland—flowers and plants played a role that was initially born of a need to clothe and feed and then bloomed into something greater

Painting on barn door in Łowicz region.

over the centuries. They became intertwined with the religion, music, dress, everyday objects and the healing arts of the people in a very deep and lasting way.

CHAPTER II

Brief History of Medicine and the Healing Arts in Poland

At about the same time as the inhabitants of the Biskupin settlement in Poland were actively using coltsfoot and tansy, Hippocrates (460 to 370 B.C.) was reputedly assembling a list of several hundred healing herbs. The ancient Greeks were already using herbs, not just for healing purposes, but in all facets of their lives. From there, the Greek's uses of herbs traveled to Rome where they were enthusiastically embraced and used, not only for medicinal purposes, but in all aspects of life. The Romans bathed in herbally scented waters, made herb pillows to induce sleep and liberally used it to enhance the food that was the cornerstone of their opulent feasts.

As civilization continued to develop, so did the knowledge of herbs and its dissemination. In 60 A.D., Dioscordes' wrote his classic text *De Materia Medica* which recorded cures involving approximately six hundred plants. It remained the principal source of information for Western physicians, including those in Poland, until the 16th century. Galen (131-199 A.D.) contributed his particular findings on medicinal plants. He wrote extensively about the body's four "humors": blood, phlegm, black bile and yellow bile. His books became the standard medical texts of the Romans, and the later Arab and medieval physicians throughout Poland and all of Europe.

After the decline of the Holy Roman Empire, the world entered a period called the Dark Ages which brought all scientific research and writing to a halt. Right around this time in Poland, King Mieszko I accepted Christianity, but pagan practices of revering trees and the elements as well as the prevailing beliefs of the causes of illness did not stop. These beliefs continued for a long time and traces of these early practices can still be found in many Polish customs and traditions today.

Woodcut depicting physician, apothecary and herb woman, from Spiczynski's "Ogród Zdrowia," 1542.

Throughout the approximate six centuries defined as the Dark Ages, European and Polish herbal traditions were not completely submerged or eradicated. A very important role was played by wanderers and itinerant merchants and peddlers from the south and east who passed through Poland. Located at the center of major trade routes from east and west, Poland saw many wanderers and travelers who had witnessed new methods of healing or heard of new plants in their travels and found ears only too willing to listen and then carry the news to others.

In Poland, as in all the rest of Europe, it was the monasteries that managed to keep alive the literature of herbs and healing practices.

Monasticism made its first appearance in Poland with the Benedictines at Międzyrzecz near Poznan and at Tyniec near Cracow in the early 11th century. In the 12th century the Cistercians arrived followed by the mendicant orders in the 13th. It was they who preserved what knowledge was known by copying manuscripts, writing their own herbals, maintaining contact with other monasteries throughout Europe, as well as cultivating and exchanging plants.

Early Health and Illness Beliefs

By the 14th century, the works of Dioscordes and Pliny were well known in Cracow, as well as the works of Galen, Hippocrates and Agricola. The Doctrine of Signatures and the hot-cold theory of illness prevailed as methods of recognizing and treating illnesses in Poland. The selection of plants and herbs used to treat a malady was governed by its similarity to the illness, adhering to the principle: like heals like. Plants with yellow flowers were used to treat jaundice while rose hips and wild strawberries were used to stimulate the blood. Headaches were treated with leaves of the waterlily due to the spherical shaped berries of the plant. If the leaves were shaped in the form of a heart, it was believed to be effective for heart ailments; if in the shape of a kidney, for kidney ailments. Those plants which grew in damp places were used to treat rheumatism. The humoral theory was used to diagnose the cause of the illness. According to this theory, the bodily humors (blood, phlegm, black bile and yellow bile) varied in both temperature and moistness. A person was healthy if there was a state of balance among these four humors which manifested itself in a wet and warm body. Illness would result from any imbalance among these humors, causing the body to become excessively dry, cold, wet or any combination of these states. The forces of nature, such as strong winds, dampness or cold air, could also have an effect on the body and cause one to become sick. Food and herbs were classified as wet or dry, hot or cold, and were used to restore the body to its natural balance.

Illness was also thought to be brought on by curses and evil looks.

Spells which caused illness and pain could be cast by supernatural beings such as witches, ghosts and water-spirits. Various epidemic diseases were believed to be caused by specific demons. Sharp stabbing pains in the spine or chest were interpreted as the result of unseen "shooting" inflicted by demons. Illnesses of the head and nerves were attributed to possession by demons. Treatment in these situations often consisted of uttering suitable magical formulas accompanied by other measures that were supposed to scare away the illness, i.e., shaking the illness out of the individual, frightening him through unexpected noises, fumigating, marking the ill area and transferring the illness to some other object. Plants and herbs that caused stinging, burning, or were bitter were also believed to be able to frighten away an illness.

In many instances, illness could be induced in another person through the use of the evil eye, manifesting itself through nausea, weakness, pains in the chest or head. A person with long silky hair that became matted, for example, was diagnosed as having been smitten by the evil eye. People were suspected of possessing the ability to cast the evil eye if their eyes had any unusual characteristics such as being inflamed, red or oddly piercing. Any child who was permitted to breast feed after the weaning period would develop the ability to cast the evil eye. Those most susceptible to harm were domestic animals, children, pregnant women and people about to embark on some happy enterprise such as marriage.

Early Organized Medicine

A significant event that would have far reaching effects in the development of medical knowledge in Poland was the organization of an Academy in Cracow in 1364. A medical faculty was established and a botanical nomeclature developed in the Polish language. One of the enlightened individuals studying there was Jan Stanko (1430-1493), a medical student and herbalist considered to be one of the most outstanding naturalists of the Middle Ages. The claim was based upon

Woodcut depicting preparation of herbs, from Spiczynski's "Ogród Zdrowia," 1542.

Stanko's authorship of a dictionary known as the *Antibolomenum* of 1472. It defined approximately 500 different plants, most of which were indigenous to Poland, and about twenty thousand alphabetical words relating to plants, written not only in German and Polish, but in other languages as well including both Latin and Greek.

POLISH HERBS, FLOWERS & FOLK MEDICINE

While the field of medicine began to grow, it took a long time to reach the general populous. The knowledge of plants and herbs began gaining a wider audience only after the onset of the availability of books. One of the first books to reach the public was written in 1537 with the work of Szymon (Simon) of Łowicz, who had studied in Italy at the Academy of Padua and later became a professor at the Academy in Cracow. His book was called *Zielnik Polski* (Polish Herbal) and illustrated with beautiful woodcuts. Following in his footsteps was Marcin Siennik, who wrote a very popular illustrated work on medicinal plants entitled *Lekarstwo Doświadczone* (Tried Medicines) which was printed in 1564. Marcin of Urzędow was another interesting individual of the times. He completed studies at the Academies of Padua and Cracow but later settled in Sandomierz as a monk where he became renowned as an excellent healer of the local people. His work was titled *Herbarz Polski, to jest o przyrodzeniu ziół y drzew rozmaitych, y innych rzeczy do lekarstw nalezacych* (Polish Herbarium, or the nature of various plants and trees and others belonging among medicine). This book appeared in print in 1595, twenty-two years after the author's death and soon became very popular. Its greatest value was that it was written completely in Polish in a lively and interesting style. It also contained information about the geographical distribution of plants. For instance: gentian—"grows high in the mountains near Sącz in the Tatra mountains and on the Babia mountains in great profusion"; or sword lily—"commonly grows in meadows and wet fields, near Cracow and grows abundantly in the meadows near St. Salvator."

Another Polish author on herbs was Szymon Syreński (1540-1611) also called Syreniusz. Syreniusz came from a town near Cracow where he completed studies at the Academy with degrees in philosophy and medicine. He then wandered throughout Europe for a time and later finished as a professor at his Alma Mater. He wrote a 1540 page herbal containing 650 excellent woodcuts that gave great details not only about plants but also about minerals and animals. It was a work of natural science which he dedicated to doctors, apothecaries, surgeons, dyers, veterinarians, grooms, gardeners, cooks, tavern-owners, farmers, wet-nurses and, finally, to lords, ladies and "anyone who had an interest."

POLISH GARDENS OF THE PAST

It was a conglomeration of the knowledge of the times, filled with prescriptions, superstitions and magic of the day. Called *O przyrodzeniu i użycie zioł* (About the properties and uses of plants), it became the first popular book on herbs. Every plant in his book was throughly explored and explained including natural habitat, soil requirements, different varieties and their uses.

Three other individuals who made significant contributions to the study of plants and herbs in the 16th century were Hieronim Spiczyński, a medical man from Cracow, Antoni Schneeberger and Stefan Falimirz. Spiczyński wrote a very useful herbarium called *Ogród Zdrowia* (Garden of Health) that was published in 1542 and contained numerous woodcuts of the plants themselves as well as their preparation. Antoni Schneeberger was a student of Gessner, the eminent Swiss naturalist and physician. He was also a Swiss who enrolled at the Jagiellonian University in Cracow and later settled there. He became one of the city's most popular physicians and scholars as well as one of its most influential citizens. Before his death he wrote ten major works dealing with natural plants and herbs.

Stefan Falimirz left his legacy in a major work called *Herbarz to Jest, Ziół tutecznych Postronnych y Zamorskich* (Herbarium or Description of Local, Foreign and Oversees Plants).

Herbal knowledge grew tremendously during the Renaissance. In the 17th century there was a monk by the name of Michael Boym, whose father was doctor to King Zygmunt III Waza (1587-1632). Boym was among the first Europeans to research the flora of China and to learn of their use of plants in medicine. Written in Chinese and Latin, he wrote an excellent work called *Chinese Medicine*. During the time of Zygmunt III Waza, such items as pepper, ginger, cloves, and cinnamon could be found in the larger marketplaces. It was also, however, a period of political unrest and wars, all of which slowed the growth and understanding of the natural sciences considerably.

In spite of the advances occuring in the knowledge of plants and their healing properties, medical education at the Academy in Cracow during the 1600's barely existed. Historians attribute this to the fact that there were no funds, no teachers and even worse, no students. At the end of the reign of August III(1735-1763) the entire faculty consisted of two professors, neither of whom were teaching. By 1777, the faculty consisted of only one professor, Dr. Badurski, who had to postpone his lectures because of a lack of students. In his report to the Commisssion on Education he wrote:

> There are only two doctors practicing and teaching in Cracow and one of them is dean over the other. They are not teaching because who would want to be their student? By the time they learn one part of medicine they would forget the other and no one doctor can be a specialist in all parts. In this entire city there is not one hospital for the sick, there is no operating theater, no herb garden associated with the academy and the whole faculty consists of two people.

During the reign of Władysław IV (1632-1648), it is known that the court medical man documented all the healing herbs and plants used in Poland. There were 750 recognized varieties when the government began controlling pharmacies. In 1633, the Sejm (Parliament) passed a law that "no one can open a pharmacy who did not pass a required exam at the Jagiellonian University." By this time the use of herbs had become much more widespread, moving into private gardens and homes.

From the years 1732-1798, King Stanisław August Poniatowski did much to increase the study of natural sciences in Poland. Numerous botanical gardens arose which continued to popularize knowledge about plants. It was during this time that Father Krzysztof Kluk (1786-1788) of Ciechanow, wrote a three volume work on herbs called the *Dictionary of Plants*.

Towards the end of the reign of King Poniatowski, the first medical school was formed in Warsaw in 1789 but it too suffered. Formal education was very expensive and lengthy. As a result, it was not surprising that there arose a great many uneducated practitioners who practiced medicine without a proper diploma. Anyone was allowed to treat patients, as long as the patient was willing. At this time there also existed a very thin line between physicians and barber-surgeons. The

Woodcut of interior of pharmacy in Poland, from Spiczynski's "Ogród Zdrowia," 1542.

barber-surgeons had their own guild, a set of by-laws, their own students and were commonly seen practicing all over Poland. They had the right to treat wounds, perform surgeries and blood-letting, set broken bones and treat sprained muscles and prepare ointments. However, they often overstepped their boundaries and dabbled in treating internal illnesses: the province of the physician.

There were also many foreign practitioners circulating in the larger cities of Poland. Some were invited by the rich and others came on their own, attracted by easy prey. The ads in the *Warsaw Gazette* from the second half of the 1700's give an idea of the level of competence of some of these so called doctors. There was Cyrus, a historian to a Prussian king who practiced ophthamology on the side, prescribing various medications that would improve short-sightedness. Then there was Prevost, a nephew and student of Bourdet, dentist of a French king, who treated scurvy, boils and infections of teeth and gums by "taking a tooth from the mouth of one person and putting it into another." He also liked to "take out the hurting tooth, fill it with lead and put it back in such a way that it will stay there." There was a chemist named Embry who used an oil made out of snake tongues to cure the thyroid, whiten the skin, strengthen the hair and kill lice. It is also worth mentioning that executioners practiced medicine and were widely accepted. The death sentence, as well as tortures, were very popular at this time. The executioners and their assistants became skillful in treating the wounds that they themselves had inflicted.

Finally, there were the quacks, magicians and self-proclaimed miracle workers who used hocus-pocus to cure people and were universally quite popular. These individuals often came to a busy town on market days and set themselves up as healers. A potential patient would be told to write the words "Abra-Kadabra" so that it filled an entire piece of paper, writing from the edges and then moving towards the center. The person had to swallow the card, drink cold water and then simply wait to be healed. Another charlatan drained three drops of blood from the large finger of the right hand; he then cut three hairs from the top of the big toe on the right foot. This was mixed together and hidden in the stump of a tree. The patient was then smeared with a salve and counseled to be tolerant for six months at which time a cure would be effected. Even though these so-called healers were recognized as fakes, they were often sought out more than properly educated physicians. Their fame and usage spread widely through all classes of people.

The largest class of healers was comprised of folk doctors and folk healers who had witnessed many illnesses during their lifetime. Their treatments included herbs, poultices and diet. When all else failed they were not above resorting to the use of hocus-pocus themselves. Many of them were ex-soldiers who had traveled widely, and had experience in treating wounds and broken bones. There were also many women who knew their herbs, helped with births and advised in the treatment of internal illnesses. It was the poor who generally availed themselves of the folk healer, however, the rich also sought their services if word got around that their cures were helpful.

The wealthier manor homes, castles and palaces often had their own still room and small pharmacy. The lady of the manor, a maiden aunt or housekeeper, collected her own herbs and distilled her own medications. She administered them not only to her family but also to the peasants and serfs who worked the manor lands. This home pharmacopeia consisted chiefly of plants and herbs of domestic origin and dozens of other ingredients. Well-stocked, it was the pride of the house. There were wine vinegars made from violets or raspberries, herbs steeped in oil, rosewater, liniments, vodka for healing and wines prepared with herbs. Added to that were dried herbs and fats from different animals to make salves and ointments. Much of their knowledge was learned firsthand from their mothers and grandmothers. They also utilized the popular literature and material that was becoming increasingly available at the end of the 1700's.

Pharmacists practiced medicine as well. Because they worked with roots and herbs, they were often perceived as an authority on medicines. Their advice was sometimes motivated by concern but very often by what treatment was costly and could turn them a profit. The pharmacist traded not only in medicines but in foreign roots, perfume, incense, pepper, cinnamon, almonds, chestnuts, bay leaves and most importantly,

Woodcut of Polish Renaissance garden.

sugar cane. They had access to an assortment of healing plants coming from India, China and the Americas such as opium, camphor, Peruvian bark and guaiac.

Besides making ointments and pills in their laboratories, the pharmacists also prepared a variety of items that had little to do with health such as candles, various vodkas, wines, sweet liquers, fruit syrups, jams, jellies, cheeses and honey cakes. Like many other health professions, training of the pharmacist was based on an apprenticeship. They organized their own guilds and if they lacked enough members in an area to establish their own, they joined the ranks of other guilds such as that of painters, jewelers and needlepointers.

Competing with the larger city pharmacies were numerous monastic pharmacies who had been in existence from the time of the Middle Ages. There were many monks who practiced medicine, taking on the functions of doctor, barber-surgeon and pharmacist. Their education was based mostly on practice, one monk teaching another. Their chief function was to care for the sick and ailing brothers within their community but their practice often extended beyond the monastery walls. Many of the sick came to the monasteries to be healed but also to receive God's blessings. The monasteries continued to prepare medicines for their own use as well as for others. By keeping in close contact with their own orders in different countries, especially if they were a part of missions in foreign lands, they could readily obtain the more exotic roots. For example, the Jesuits were famous for selling quinine under the name *pulvis Jesuiticus*. The monastic pharmacies were sometimes utilized only for their own private use but they often served the surrounding population as well. They gave away medicines for free to both poor and rich or sold them for profit, depending on the needs of the order. The city and town pharmacies, threatened by decreased profits, petitioned religious authorities to limit the commercial activities of the monastic pharmacies. Religious authorities complied. In a memorandum written in 1629, the head of the Jesuits forbade the sale of medicines and allowed dispensing of free medication only to the poor. Some obeyed this order and some did not. When the pope intervened and forbade newly ordained monks from practicing medicine, many of the men simply continued to live among the brothers, never accepting holy orders—allowing them to continue practicing medicine and running pharmacies.

Medicines were also distributed by traveling salesmen, often from Hungary, called *Węgier* (Hungarian). They carried packs on their shoulders filled with herbs and ointments. This included Hungarian pepper for headaches or remedies for infertility, as well as various soaps and perfumes. It was inevitable that these homegrown traveling salesmen became both physican and pharmacist, diagnosing people's complaints and prescribing a remedy from the bag of goodies strapped to their back. So prolific were these traveling salesmen that Princess Elizabeth Sapieżyna issued an edict in 1774 for the town of Koźmin to stop traveling salesmen from selling their products.

Over time, literacy increased in Poland and herbals and their remedies became available to everyone. In 1892, a priest by the name of Sebastian Kneipp published a popular herbal with drawings of plants called *Herbal* or *Atlas of Healing Plants*. When thousands of Poles left overcrowded parts of Poland for new lands in America, they brought this book with them as well as roots and slips of the plants they considered essential to their health and well-being. They continued to use their knowledge of herbs as the first method of treatment for any aches, pains or illnesses they experienced. Studies of early Polonia, Polish-American communities in America, reveal that herb stores were very common and did a large volume of business.

There are two other men who must be mentioned for their more current and significant contributions to documenting and preserving folk medicine and healing practices in Poland. One was Dr. Marjan Udziela who wrote *Medycyna i Przesądy Lecznicze Ludu Polskiego* (Medicine and Folk Beliefs of the People of Poland) in 1891 and Jan Muszyński (1884-1957), a professor of pharmacology as well as the author of a very popular text on herbal medicine that circulated throughout Poland called *Ziołolecznictwo i Leki Roślinne* (Herbology and Healing Plants) in 1946.

CHAPTER III

Polish Gardens of the Past

The Monastery Garden

And what are garden beds? Windows to heaven...
In the flower, God is mystically veiled
as under a gilded canopy,
while an ensemble of nightingales chant his praises.
—Dominik Rudnicki (1676-1739)
Jesuit Society of Jesus

The oldest examples of preserved medieval gardens in Poland are located within monasteries and around castles. The monastery courtyard, called a cloister, was founded on the notion of the Roman *carum aedium* that is, a small enclosed garden incorporating an atrium and peristyle. After the fall of the Holy Roman Empire, it managed to survive in architecture chiefly due to the Byzantine church. The first European monasteries adopted the architectural pattern for their own. While limiting contact with the outside world, the cloister still provided the monks with their much desired contact with nature.

The cloister consisted of a complex of four buildings joined together at the corners to form a small internal rectangular courtyard. Open to the sun and air, it was surrounded by the walls of the church on one side, the refectory on another and two other buildings. At the center of this courtyard was generally a well, a fountain or a tree. There were paths radiating away from the center diagonally, horizontally and/or vertically. Often a stone bench offered a brief respite from labors. In between the paths, herbs were cultivated and flowers grown by the sacristan to adorn the church, shrines and statues. It was here that monks

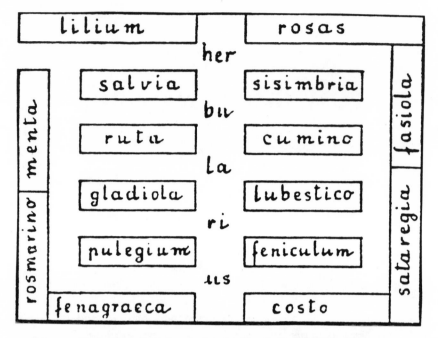

Drawing of herb garden at St. Gall (Benedictine).

came to meditate, to study or to take their recreation while walking along the paths between the narrow beds of herbs and flowers. Dynastic changes, conquests, and plagues shook the foundations of civilized life yet the cloister offered silence, contact with nature and serenity from a sometimes hostile and warring world. Polish historians write: "through the cloisters we come to understand the gardens of the times: marjoram, basil, sage, rue, violets, carnations, lilies, roses, irises, southernwood, rosemary, lavender, spikenard and others."

Monasticism made its first appearance in Poland in the 11th century with the Benedictines from Monte Cassino and Cluny in France. They settled at Międzyrzecz near Poznan and at Tyniec, the main abbey, near Cracow in the early 11th century and spread throughout Poland over the succeeding generations, each having its own church and hospital. The Benedictine rule prescribed manual labor, generally agricultural labor, for an average of seven hours a day. Herbs were grown in the physic (medicinal) garden, vegetable and cooking herbs in the kitchen garden

48

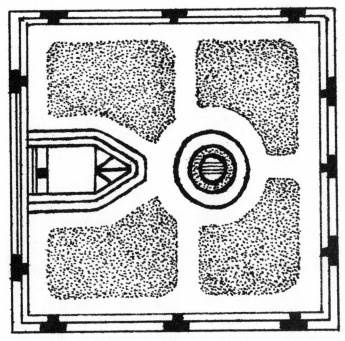

Cloister at Oliva (Cistercian).

and flowers and herbs in the ornamental gardens for decorating the church altars. A well documented plan preserved at the Abbey of St. Gall in Switzerland, dating from 820-830 AD, shows in great detail how a major religious institution should be laid-out according to the rule of St. Benedict as a self-contained and self-sufficient community with farms, orchards and gardens. The St. Gall plan was copied in many monastery courtyards including the ones in Poland at Mogiła, Oliwa, and Sulejów. Besides the cloister courtyard, there were other cultivated gardens—orchards and vegetable gardens—laid-out with walkways and rest areas. The garden beds were arranged in square or rectanglular shapes and divided by walkways. They were planted with fruit trees, vegetables, and culinary and medicinal herbs. The plan contained a physician's house with its own infirmary garden of sixteen beds labeled with their herbal occupant, among which were rose, cumin, lovage, fennel, lilies, sage, pennyroyal, fenugreek, mint and rosemary. In larger holdings, there were also vineyards and hop-gardens. The entire property was surrounded by a high brick wall.

In the 12th century the Cistercians arrived in Poland from France. The Cistercians settled in Poland at Mogiła outside of Cracow in the 12th century, building a magnificent church and fortified monastery. The monastery had a beautiful cloistered garden and the abbey was surrounded by extensive gardens. The layout of Polish Cistercian monasteries was similar to the French motherhouses in Clairvaux and Citeux. Their rule also required that they be involved with agriculture and gardening. As a result, Cistercian monks were the best agronomists, stock breeders and foresters of the latter Middle Ages. They were also experts in the use of water. They generally settled in low-lying, fertile areas near rivers where the water aided growth and production. Such monasteries were established at Mogiła, Sulejów, Jędrzejów and Koprzywnica. The Cistercian monks attacked marshes, poor soil and impenetrable undergrowth with joy and zeal, succeeding to the point where they owned vast estates and whole villages sprang up around them. At their monastery at Mogiła, established in 1222 on the river Dłubnia, they not only gardened but also ran paper mills and fulleries, exporting their products to all parts of Europe.

The hermit orders, such as the Carthusians and Cameldolite, in accordance with their by-laws, maintained minimal contact with others. Their monastaries were built to accomodate these rules. In contrast to the Benedictines, they lived enclosed lives, never leaving the monastery. Established near Gdansk in 1381, the monastery buildings significantly resembled the motherhouse in Clermont, France. They created a regular quadrangle around a large cloister with a cemetery at the center. The Carthusians lived in seperate cells, each of which opened up into its own small, private garden growing food, herbs and flowers. Carthusian monks soon became involved in exporting herbs that they themselves had grown.

It was near the monasteries that hospitals and herb gardens were first established in Poland and where the monks prepared "foreign medicine." The first apothecary/pharmacy existed at the Benedictine Monastery at Holy Cross in the beginning of the 12th century. The common language of Latin, their high literacy, and shared interests in horticulture and healing, led to numerous exchanges of information on plants, their use and culture. This information was often laboriously copied by the monks into their herbals and brought to other countries as their orders grew.

By the Middle Ages, monks were dispensing medicinal herbs and providing overnight lodgings for travelers, including pilgrims who both supplied them with medicinal practices seen on their travels and who conveyed messages between monasteries. Monasteries began to expand significantly and their gardens grew in proportion with the increasing size of their buildings and the number of inhabitants. Besides the cloister, which was still at the heart of each monastery, there were herb gardens or physic gardens for healing the sick brethren as well as ailing folks who came to the monasteries to be treated. In the physic garden, various healing herbs were raised: sage, rue, mint, angelica, wormwood and others. Large vegetable gardens and orchards were needed to feed the growing number of monks, pilgrims and visiting dignitaries that crossed the monastery gates. These larger gardens and orchards were situated beyond the monastery buildings, but always enclosed by a wall. By the 12th century, in Śląsk, Wielkopolska and Sandomierz, monasteries were expanding significantly beyond herbs and orchards to establish their own vineyards for the making of sacramental wines.

Castles, Villa and Manor Gardens

It was the kitchen garden. Row on row
Of fruit trees give their shade to beds below.
—Pan Tadeusz

To know Polish history is to know a history of warring, of boundaries expanding and contracting, of conquering and being conquered. For centuries, Poland's flat, rolling lands with no natural defenses, made it a prime target for a host of foreign invaders including the Swedes, Turks and Mongol hordes. The time of the Dark Ages was an especially significant period of unrest and warring in Poland as well as throughout the rest of Europe. The constant strife and warfare led to the building of enormous castles and fortified structures to protect against raiding armies. These early Polish castles were built on high ground with natural defensive advantages. Oftentimes, space within the walls was limited to that needed for appropriate fortification of the castle. In Poland, as in other European countries of the time, under favorable conditions there was a small decorative garden called *a hortus conclusis*, arranged near the living space of the owner or the women's quarters. According to custom, it was surrounded by a high wall, similar to a cloister at a monastery. It was here, within the protected confines of the castle, that the women came to enjoy fair weather, ply their needles or gather flowers and herbs to make into simples. It was a sanctuary, a private place where decorative flowers and bushes were planted, especially the rose, which was a favorite in Polish gardens during these dark and troubled times.

Sometimes the *hortus conclusis* contained a tree such as linden, oak or maple to provide shade. Seats under trees were a particular feature of these early castle gardens. Many illustrations of the gardens of the time depict seats of brick, stone or wattle supporting a turf top. The castle of Melsztyn, established on a lofty crag over the Dunajec, in spite of limited room, contained both a small decorative garden for the women of the castle, and a hop-garden for the making of beer.

In light of the universal custom of growing rose bushes in the *hortus conclusis*, it was also called the rose garden. It would have a well or fountain, depending on the financial means of the owner. The *hortus conclusis* was often a theme in Polish religious paintings of the 15th and 16th centuries, depicting the Madonna and Child with a garden in the background.

Other necessary gardens for the feeding of the castle inhabitants, such as vegetables gardens or orchards were entirely dependent on the castle's surroundings. Very often they were not one collective body, but were dispersed here and there depending on the terrain and quality of the soil. If the castle was built on a steep hill, the gardens were established somewhere on a softer slope. Castle inventories still in existence indicate "vineyard on the hill near the castle surrounded by a wattle and blackthorn fence...a garden near the castle for vegetables in which there is an apple and plum tree."

Another interesting castle inventory that has been preserved from this particular era is the account books of King Jagiello and his wife, Queen Hedwig, during the years 1388-1420. They contained the list of everyday expenses for palace needs and gave a sense of the foods and plants that were grown on the king's estate. Besides the usual grains of oats, wheat and rye, lentils also figured strongly. Fruits from the king's orchard yielded pears, plums and cherries. Vegetables included pumpkins, carrots, beets, cabbage, radishes and onions. Herbs listed were bishop's weed, black mustard, hemp, dill, poppy, and parsley.

The Italian Influence

In the 13th century, Petrus de Crescentiis of Bologna, Italy wrote a book on husbandry in which he distinguished between small gardens and those of the wealthy, indicating that larger gardens were coming into being. The larger garden was enclosed behind a high wall. "Towards the north," said Crescentiis, "there should be a thicket of tall trees where wild beasts are kept and to the south a palace with shady trees and an aviary. In other parts there should be shrubberies in which the tamer animals should be kept, but not placed so as to obscure the view from the palace. There should be a summer house, made from trained trees, over which vines could be allowed to trail. The ground should be ornamented with evergreens carefully placed and there should be clipped trees cut out as walls, palisades and turrets."

The influence of Crescentiis, and his ideas for gardening, spread throughout the west and requests for Italian gardeners to exercise their skill in other countries were received. Peter de Crescentiis, was known in Poland as Krescentyn. His work was translated into Polish by Andzej Trzycieski and published in Cracow. It became very popular in Poland as a textbook and was used as one of the chief resources for gardening "in the Italian style." As the centuries advanced, strongly fortified castles designed wholly for battle ceased to be built. Castles became less fortress-like, defense walls were removed and gardens became more elaborate. They were no longer small plots with a few plants, but now comprised of large cultivated areas which included beds arranged in ornamental patterns and menageries. Cracow began to expand under a more peaceful time.

Cracow and Łobzów

Cracow had been the capital of Poland since 1083. By the 14th century, it contained a medieval castle called Wawel, built by the Piast family (the early rulers of Poland) and was a major residence of the senior royalty of Poland. Following the trends of the times, King Kazimierz the Great (1333-1370) built himself a small castle/hunting lodge called Łobzów near Cracow in 1357. Today that region has been incorporated into the city, but at that time it was one of the summer residences where royal hunts were held.

The residence was similar to the early Renaissance villas which were designed for rest and relaxation and subsequently built away from the city. Influenced by trends from Italy, elaborate knot gardens and parterres were established which Kazimierz, in true kingly style, enjoyed with his string of mistresses. A children's street song from the times proclaims the King's use of his garden: "Near a garden bed at Łobzów, Kazimierz the Great drinks mead with Esther."

Accounts still extant indicate that at the garden in Łobzów "there are knot gardens with the coat of arms made from boxwood...around the knot gardens, a fence in the new French mode...a labyrinth garden...there are also fig trees." Later in 1585, under King Stefan Batory, the garden supposedly had three knot gardens for herbs like roses, rosemary, lavender, spikenard, pinks and violets and twelve gardens for grapevines and fruit trees. In the courtyard there was a raised turf seat for individuals to sit on and take their leisure as well as other trees to provide shade and coolness. From the south and west side, the garden was planted with trees because it is from this side that "dark and unhealthy winds blow." On the other side of the garden, there was a pond surrounded by lindens. Eight gardeners were required to maintain the garden.

The garden at Łobzów was gradually enlarged by Italian architects Santi Gucci and Giovanni Trevano and became what was considered perhaps the most beautiful garden in Poland and where Queen Bona, King Henry of Valois and the papal legate, Gaetano, started their ceremonial processions before entering Cracow.

In 1655, the Swedes completely plundered the castle at Łobzów which was then restored by King Jan II Sobieski. In 1777, King Stanisław Augustus bequeathed the palace and the garden to Cracow University and in 1850, when most of southern Poland was under Austrian rule, it was turned into an army barracks. Not much of the former splendour of the castle has survived, and the gardens have disappeared without a trace.

Wawel Castle

At the royal castle at Wawel in Cracow, there existed a decorative garden within the castle walls. "With the advent of spring and the blossoming of violets and roses," wrote Pawinski about the young King Zygmunt I, "the king delights in the smell of the flowers in the garden." Later, this same king, called Zygmunt the Old (1467-1548) allowed his ailing wife Barbara the luxury of an herb and flower garden within the castle walls because she, "For health purposes, wanted to walk in the royal gardens." She died in 1515 and was followed by Bona Sforza, who came to Poland in 1518.

Queen Bona Sforza, second wife of Zygmunt I, was from the Italian Sforza d'Aragon family and the daughter of Duke Gian Galeazzo Sforza of Milan and Isabella of Aragon. According to some historians, she was one of the most illustrious women ever to sit on the throne of Poland. Queen Bona surrounded herself with her Italian countrymen and the Italian ways of thinking and acting spread quickly throughout Poland, contributing significantly to the Renaissance in Poland.

Under her influence, the city of Cracow became the cradle of "Italian gardens" in Poland. Queen Bona immediately established at Wawel a small Italian garden, vineyard and dove cote for her daughters' pleasure. The Italian architects eventually rebuilt the much neglected Wawel Castle and the Cathedral. Queen Bona also introduced a model agricultural economy that included the cultivation of cauliflower and tomatoes, set up orchards and vegetable farms and built scores of castles each with gardens for pleasure and for consumption.

Garden at the Royal Castle in Warsaw

On May 25, 1609, the capital of Poland was moved from Cracow to Warsaw. On the steep slope of the escarpment which overlooked the Wisła River, an Italian style garden with geometrically arranged flower beds and pruned plants was founded in the middle of the 16th century by Queen Bona and later looked after by Anna the Jagiellonian. After the death of her husband, the widowed Queen Bona resided in Ujazdów, a village not far from Warsaw on the picturesque Wisła escarpment. It was built in the Italian style—a *villa suburbana*—surrounded by a large garden with regularly laid out flower beds and vegetation in geometrical shapes. Caligari, the papal nuncio, who saw the Ujazdów residence in 1580, admired its beautiful location over the Wisła and its Italian-style gardens and also liked: "The palace which is completely made of wood, a local custom, but still beautiful."

In the course of the following centuries the garden at the royal palace went through several alterations. During the 17th century, exotic trees in large pots were placed on the edge of the escarpment and a small garden with six flower beds was established on a flat triangular area by the southeast wing. There were sculptures, fountains and even ornamental bird cages. In 1650, the wife of King Jan founded a botanical garden which acquired some fame. Simon Paulli wrote about it in his *Viridaria varia regia et academia publica...*, published in Copenhagen in 1653. The book mentions that there were 737 species of plants in the castle garden. At that time, the royal garden in Paris had 2,121 species and the Oxford University garden had 1,472. The castle garden was also described by the court botanist Jan Kazimierz Marcin Bernitz.

In 1737, Gaetano Chiaveri designed a new garden in the French Baroque style with regularly shaped flower beds spread out in the slope of the escarpment. In the 19th century the garden was transformed into a romantic landscape design with luxuriant flora which hid the architecture of the castle on the Wisła side in an unsuitable way. It remained this way until it was recreated it in a style appropriate to the 18th century.

Renaissance Period

The Renaissance Period (1450-1600) saw tremendous economic and cultural expansion in Poland. Poland's varied dynastic and trade contacts with Western and Southern Europe brought to Cracow, chiefly in the 16th century, a great multitude of completely unknown plants especially fruits and vegetables and medicines. Italian fruits, such as oranges, lemons, pomegranates, olives, figs, chestnuts, raisins and almonds and spices such as pepper, fennel, saffron, ginger, nutmeg, cloves, and cinnamon were brought from abroad by various routes via Nuremberg, Wrocław or Venice and Vienna. The Polish envoy to Turkey brought back tobacco seeds that were planted in castle gardens. Seeds of paprika and maize were also brought in from that country. Travelers brought home other useful plants such as the potato which, rejected initially, became the mainstay of consumption for the majority of peasants. Flowers such as fritillaria imperialis (tulip), lilac, sunflower, spiderwort, larkspur and a host of others were entering Poland from foreign countries. The Dutch influence in gardening was felt very strongly in the north in Gdansk and Sczeczin. Herbs and plants were being imported from the Netherlands both for medicinal and decorative purposes. They were imported through Gdansk which had a monopoly on the handling of seeds for the entire Baltic region. Dutchman Vredman de Vries

Dutch influence on Polish Knot gardens.

authored a book of designs on knot gardens and parterres. He also helped popularize the fashioning of topiaries in geometric, animal and human shapes.

Simultaneously, the Viennese gardening firm of Jan Helda and Jan Hendera advertised in Polish journals that seeds for practically all vegetables could be had including broccoli, basil, spanish onion and endive. Among the wealthy, the costlier imported flowers could be seen: tulips, narcissus and hyacinths. The French influence became very popular in Warsaw as the new capital of Poland. Private gardens were flourishing and foreign plants were eagerly collected and cultivated. Interest in medicine grew. The first botanical gardens were founded for comprehensive collection. A great number of herbals were being published and knot gardens became increasingly popular in Poland, not only in royal residences but among nobles and even the well-to-do merchants.

Polish Knot Gardens

A knot garden was an ornamental garden bed laid out in patterns using low evergreen bushes or scented herbs. The knot garden was almost always designed in a square framework with flowers or herbs grown within the edging. Lavender, thyme, rosemary, cotton lavender and hyssop have been used for edging in Polish knot patterns since the 15th century.

Knot gardens evolved from medieval kitchen gardens where separate beds contained medicinal and cooking herbs to prevent confusion. In early gardens the flowers and herbs were always used to fill in the pattern but later when gardens became purely ornamental, the hedges themselves became the design focus and the spaces between them were filled with earth, sand, brick or coal dust to enhance the pattern.

The writer and chronicler Mikołaj Rej (1505-1569), the first poet to describe Polish life in the Polish language, drew up a very careful recommendation on "how a man should with his wife and household walk in orchards and gardens, graft little shoots and plant little trees." Or else the man could "with great delight plant herbs, radishes, lettuces and cress, or nice melons, cucumbers, marjoram, sage and other herbs." Imparting this culinary advice, Rej also refers to knot gardens in Poland: "The green grove planted round with roses, with red and white bushes gracefully alternating; where rosemary, marjoram, lavender, spikenard, hyssop, lilies and peonies stand in their rows and between them violets, lovely daisies and lilies of the valley. Both are surrounded by juniper." The chief plant used to frame the knot garden was juniper bush and boxwood. At that time, roses played a major role in flower gardens. Second in importance were violets, lilies, peonies and dianthus which had maintained their popularity from the times of the Middle Ages.

There are few extant drawings of old knot gardens from this period. However, some from the Cameldolite monastery at Bielany just outside

Old knot garden designs at monastery at Bielany in Cracow.

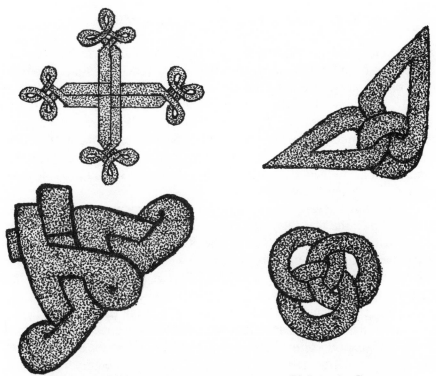

Old knot garden designs at monastery at Bielany in Cracow.

of Cracow still exist. The monastery was built by an Italian architect in the years 1622-1644.

17th and 18th Century Gardens

During these centuries, Polish gardens were heavily influenced by any rage blowing through the gardening world. It was a time when the aristocracy was giving much attention to their gardens. Roses were being imported from France, lilies from Turkey and massive gardens were being styled in the classical, baroque and romantic style by kings and nobles.

At the beginning of the 17th century, the Italian influence was at its peak in Poland. In 1618, the poet Slupski recommended "the skillful gardener to plant herbs agreeable to the master, to form the pleasure gardens into laid-out squares, to produce pleasant forms and sundials from boxwood, where delighful flowers of the tulip could be planted."

In the latter half of the century, King Jan Sobieski III (1629-1696), the famous victor of the Battle of Vienna, built himself a summer residence outside of Warsaw on the Wisła River, and called it an Italian *villa nuova* (hence the name Wilanów). Behind the residence he established a two level Italian garden decorated with gilded mythological figures, vases and fountains.

King Jan Sobieski shared an interest in gardening with his wife, Maria. While she was busying herself establishing the botanical garden at the King's Palace in Warsaw, the King was indulging himself at Wilanów planting his own trees. It is he who is credited with bringing the chestnut tree and Chinese cedar to Poland as well as bringing the Italian poplar from Turkey. It is also to his credit that he brought the potato plant to Poland in 1615 and had it planted in the royal gardens.

After the death of Jan Sobieski, Wilanów changed hands many times and numerous alterations were introduced both to the buildings and the gardens. In the last two decades of the 18th century, the royal residence was the home of the very rich and powerful Potocki family. The owner Stanisław Kostka Potocki enlarged the gardens and transformed them into an English-style landscape park decorated with summer houses and structures, then in great vogue.

In the 18th century Poland was overtaken by a penchant for the classical. It was promoted by King August II Mocny (1670-1733) who built a mighty palace and magnificent French-style Saxon garden called Ogród Saski in Warsaw. Built on forty two acres of land on a trapezoidal plan, it was styled after the French landscape gardener Andre Le Nôtre who believed in massive scale, infinite vistas and elaborate parterres. Parterres were gardens developed as flat, open terraces. It is a word adapted from *broderie par terre*, or embroidery on the ground. Boxwood acted as the stitching, so to speak, to create a design on the ground. The style became favored by nobles such as the Lubomirski and Potocki with their gardens at Łancut and Krystynopol. Immense stretches of green lawn, large pools of water enclosed in regularly shaped basins, and trees and shrubs cut down to geometrical figures became the desired garden look of the wealthy. Polish poet and satirist Ignacy Krasicki (1735-1801) complained: "That gardener was considered the best master of his art who could most elaborately shear trees, make them crooked, low or tall, lop them, broaden them out and pull them into shape."

In the second half of that century another new philosophical and asthetic trend emerged in Britain and France, influencing Polish gardening. Taking their inspiration from the traditions of the classical world and the Middle Ages, the propagators of the new philosophy called for a return to the past and to nature. In their writings, Jean Jacques Rousseau, the French philosopher and writer, and Alexander Pope in England called for a return to nature and chastised all that was not natural. They praised nature as innately good and advocated gardens grown informally. These fashionable ideas did not take long to inspire the leisured women of the foremost Polish families. The rich women of the Czartoryski, Lubomirski and Radziwiłł families rushed to create their own nature parks.

It was Izabella Czartoryska, daughter of the renowned and fabulously wealthy Prince Adam Czartoryski, who popularized English gardens in Poland. She penned a book called *Various Thoughts on the Creation of Gardens* which was published in 1805. Scorning the previous mode of precise shaping, she stated: "Forms forced on trees are in my opinion, abominable, cut down to the form of columns, or globes or expanded into fans, they truly do not adorn any place. If a son inherits them from his father in such a form, he had best not touch them and allow nature, in the course of time, to rehabilitate and reclothe them." While the previous classical period in gardening advocated symmetry and elegance in its design, the new, romantic style encouraged the opposite, to design freely without any attempt at regularity and symmetry, to be sentimental and pastoral. The style called for a picturesque site filled with greenery, thatched huts, bee-gardens, a farmyard, grottos, clocktowers and romantic Swiss or Dutch cottages. "In every cottage," wrote Izabella Czartoryska, "a resident should be established. If we consider the view, then it will be enlivened by an inhabited house; if we think of pleasure, it is most pleasant when

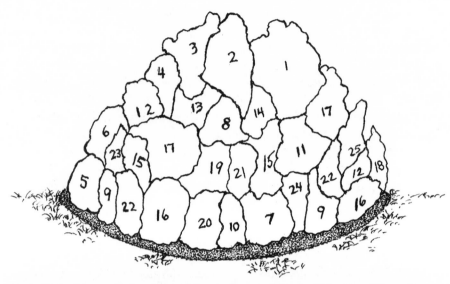

Isabella's flower bed, adapted from Czartoryska's "Various Thoughts on the Creation of Gardens."

1. Rose
2. Hollyhock
3. Coreopsis verticullata
4. Veronica martina
5. Digitalis purpurea
6. Campanula medium
7. Ibiris umbellata
8. Campanula speculum
9. Tagetes patula
10. Vinca major
11. White impatiens
12. Monarda didyma
13. Calendula officinalis
14. Convolvolus tricolor
15. Juniperus sabina
16. Tropacolum minus
17. Phlox paniculata
18. Solanum dulcamara
19. Acheilla ptarmia
20. Cheiranthus martimus
21. Saponaria officinalis
22. Fritillaria corona imperialis
23. Impatiens (rose colored)
24. Lily
25. Trachelium caeraleum

entering a hut to find the tenant and his wife gay and happy." With the help of English landscape gardener James Savage (1740-1816) and the outstanding Polish architect Chrystian Piotr Aigner (1756-1842), she established a beautiful romantic landscape park in Puławy near Lublin that took forty years to complete. Along the top of an escarpment, specially planted trees accented park buildings such as the Temple of Sybil, a Gothic House, Fisherman's House, Dutch House, Chinese pavilions, and marble sarcophagi. Lakes and long drives were bordered by rows upon rows of linden trees. A sketch from her book offers a flower bed that provides color throughout the summer.

The most original and unusual park connected with the romantic period was Arkadia. Commissioned by Princess Helena Radziwiłł, the park was designed by Szymon Bogumił Zug, court architect to King Poniatowski. According to the princess it was to be an "idyllic land of peace and happiness." The park was named after the Arcadian myth containing symbols of happiness, love and death. She began the park around 1780 and it underwent constant improvements until her death in 1821. The pastoral and bucolic look she sought came at a great cost. She traveled extensively and sent home columns from Italy, artifical ruins and grottos, a magnificent Roman aqueduct with two tiers of arcades, tombstones and statues, antique sculptures and exotic works of art. There were traces of Greek and Roman grandeur with a Roman circus or arena for chariot races, granite obelisks and ornaments of bronze and marble. Helena Radziwiłł also created an island in the center of a lake on which rested a copy of the tomb of the French philospher, Rousseau. A walk encircled the lake on which could be found The Temple of Diana with its famous sphinx guarding the steps.

The names of magnificent gardens dotting the Polish landscape during these times are prodigious: Nieborów with its famous Orangery sent from Dresden, embroidered parterres and canals were established by Michał Hieronim Radziwiłł and his wife Helena of the Arkadia fame; the *elegantissima* gardens with knot gardens made of six-pointed stars, herb gardens and orangery of Kryżtopór in a small village called Ujazd built by the governor of the Sandomierz province; Łazienki, summer residence of King Stanisław August Poniatowski (1732-1798), built on an island in a lake looking out on a park which took twelve years of work to complete; Natolin with its Dutch Farm and Doric Temple; and Łancut with winding drives, groves of trees, small castle and menagerie.

The rage for the Chinese garden also reached Poland and exerted a strong and significant oriental influence in gardens. Polish magnates erected airy park buildings, Chinese bowers, pagodas, kiosks, little mosques, chinese bridges and Turkish fountains. When Wilanów was in the hands of the Lubomirski families, Izabella Lubomirska produced an Anglo-Chinese garden "with curved and winding paths between groups of trees and shrubs, with a murmuring cascade and picturesquely mirrored in a pond and lake beyond."

There was little in the way of gardening trends sweeping through Europe that did not make itself felt in the Polish landscape.

The Peasant Garden

Like well-kept flower beds-everyone could tell
That plenty in that house and order dwell.
—Pan Tadeusz

Great landowners, kings and nobles were not the only individuals who enjoyed gardens in Poland. Even the humblest of serfs and peasants admired the beauty of a flower and could find comfort and solace among plants. But unlike kings and wealthy nobles, whose gardens were grand and sumptuous affairs to display one's wealth and leisure, the garden for the peasant was a more simple and useful place. It was a place where roses and flowers of assorted size and shape mingled comfortably with herbs, vegetables and berry bushes. There were a few cultivated herbs for making medicine or for adding to the soup kettle. There were vegetables needed on a small scale such as radishes and onions to garnish a meal; fruit for preserving or making into jams and jellies; a profusion of favorite flowers to gladden the heart, to provide nectar for bees and to adorn the altars at church. It was the typical cottage garden.

Unlike the kitchen gardens of England and subsequently the Colonial gardens of America, the Polish cottage garden was not directly accessible from the back kitchen door. With some exceptions, the Polish peasant cottage garden was always in front of the house, facing the road

66

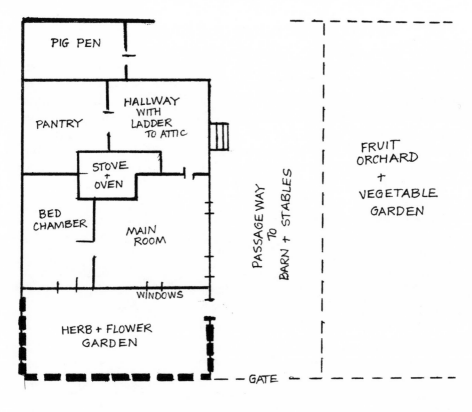

Layout of peasant cottage.

and, if possible, with a southern exposure. It was located in full view of both passers-by on the road and individuals living in the house.

Most Polish peasant cottages were situated so that the narrow end, also called the gable end, faced the street. Most plots were long and narrow, with the house in front and necessary outbuildings, such as the barn and chicken coop, located behind. Fruit and nut trees, if they could be afforded, were planted where exposure and soil seemed best. Large plots of vegetables such as beets, potatoes, cabbage and other necessary basic food staples needed in larger quantities were not always grown near the home plot but on parcels of land some distance away. The main entrance to the house was not in the front, directly from the street, but from the side where there was a lot of everyday hustle and bustle with the animals being taken to the back, hay being brought into outbuildings, etc. Subsequently, most cottage gardens were located in the front of the house where they could not only avoid being trampled but where they could be admired and appreciated by those passing by.

Chiefly the domain of the housewife and grown daughters, the ultimate purpose of the garden was to be functional in nature but it also served to make a statement. In any small village population where a social and financial hierarchy existed, flowers growing in a garden offered evidence of social superiority. It was testimony that there was enough in the house for the housewife to indulge herself in something as frivolous as growing flowers. Each housewife strove to make her garden the best that finances, free time and her own creativity would allow.

The garden was usually surrounded by a fence and accessed through a gate. The most typical type of fence surrounding the Polish cottage garden was a wooden picket or a wattle fence. The wattle fence was very popular since willow was plentiful along streams and rivers and had the added advantage of costing very little. Young flexible willow stalks were woven either horizontally or vertically between posts. In some instances the wattle fences were built high enough to keep away curious onlookers, particularly if the owner was superstitious and frightened of the evil eye. But for most intents and purposes, the fencing helped determine property boundaries and keep out stray animals.

As mentioned earlier, the cottage garden was a mix of decorative and useful herbs, vegetables, flowers and shrubs such as roses, raspberry, gooseberry, or currant bushes. There was no specific garden plan. Flowers and herbs were usually grown in clumps near the fence or in beds beneath the windows of the house according to the preferences of the housewife. Vegetables were occasionally mixed in. The walkways were made of tamped soil and wide enough for a person to walk through. If a bit of decoration was wanted, large rocks were gathered,

Picket Fences

painted white and fashioned in a circle. Inside, a special flower or herb was planted.

The housewife grew flowers to brighten the outside of the house, to adorn the altars at church on Sundays and holy days and to decorate the wayside shrines that were located within the village boundaries. The unmarried girls of the house tended lilies, rosemary and rue for bridal wreathes as well as lavender to place between the linens in her marriage chest. For cooking and to spice the daily fare, some culinary herbs were planted. There was marjoram for sausage, dill for pickling cucumbers, and parsley, sage and fennel for enhancing soups and stews. Many Polish housewives made their own herb vinegars from water and sliced apples that were allowed to ferment over a few months time. The mixture was strained, crushed herbs added, sealed in bottles and stored in a cool pantry or larder. Herb butters were also made and packed

Wattle Fence   **Clay Flower Pot**

down into crocks to use in the middle of winter or to give as a Christmas gift.

Interspersed among the flowers were vegetables such as cucumbers, radishes, water cress, horseradish and lettuce. Sometimes there were beets, carrots, garlic or onions depending on the needs and tastes of the owner. It was Queen Bona Sforza who introduced various green vegetables to Poland including beans, cabbage, cauliflower, onion, celery, parsnip, cumin, coriander, caraway, hemp, asparagus, artichoke, tomato and nasturtium. Spinach also traveled to Poland from Italy, brought by monks who followed Bona in her marriage to Zygmunt. From nearby Germany came horseradish and pumpkin, which also made its appearance in Polish cottage gardens.

There was a great deal of trading and exchanging of slips and cuttings among the village housewives. Seeds were also traded and exchanged with family and friends or, if finances allowed, bought from the traveling packman. A trip to a large city market to sell extra vegetables and herbs brought the opportunity to buy a variety of bulbs and, if it had been a good market day, the housewife could indulge in treating herself to the more exotic bulb: the tulip. Tulips, considered the highpoint of the garden, were imported into Poland through Gdansk and eventually reached even the smaller towns and villages. Even more desirable was a cultivated pear or cherry tree. Considered a real prize, such a tree was planted where early spring blossoms and the growing fruit could be viewed and enjoyed from a window.

It is important to realize that, unlike today, where scarcely a Polish home exists that does not have a fresh flower in it, it was not the general custom among Polish cottage gardeners of the previous century to bring fresh-cut flowers into the home. Fresh flowers were kept outside in the garden to beautify the house and to take to church to decorate the altars on Sundays and holy days. For inside, paper flowers were made in the shape of roses, lilies and morning glories, etc., and placed on the table or dresser. This was especially true for "God's Corner," a shelf, a table top or dresser top where the family bible, crucifix and holy water were kept. Paper flowers also decorated the tops of windows or a small bouquet of flowers held back the curtains to allow more light.

Except for such herbs as mallow, mint, and chamomile, medicinal herbs were rarely grown in large quantities in the front garden. The country woman foraged for her medicinal herbs in the meadows, fields and forests. She made many a trip to the woods with her daughters searching out plants for healing wounds and bruises, warming the stomach, easing an ear-ache or simply to bring rosiness to the cheeks. The herbs were brought home and dried in front of the fireplace hearth and in later years above the stove.

Until the late 18th century, most ordinary country dwelling families in Poland lived, cooked and ate in the same room, cooking over an open fire on the hearth with the use of a tripod. The more prosperous homes had a network of smaller rooms, larders or pantries that led off the main room. A Polish folklorist documenting the use of herbs by country women in the Poznan region noted that "in the pantry, besides barrels full of flour and bins of buckwheat groats and bags of herbs hanging from the rafters, the housewife kept a ready supply of mint, chamomile, linden, elderberry flowers, dried blueberries, and centaury in a medicine chest which consisted of many small drawers. Nearby were bottles of camphor, terpentine, brandy and a few bottles of vodka."

In a small village called Augustow in the Białystok region, one family began to document various family recipes over a period of fifty years. Besides writing down such useful information as recipes for fermenting honey into mead as well as making soap, fireproof plaster, tinctures and cheeses, there was a list of "medications required in the home." These included: chamomile, elderberry, mullein, linden flower, dried poppy flowers found growing among the grain, white mustard seeds, leaves of coltsfoot, pansy flowers, couch grass, leaves and root of mallow, sage, root of calamus, mistletoe, dried blueberries, dried sour cherries, and rhubarb. Other necessary items for a well stocked medicinal larder included honey, a strong "spirytus" (95% proof alcohol), stout vinegar, cantharides (spanish fly) gathered in May and kept in bottles, leeches, Cologne water, lavender water and a good clear wax. It also recommended buying the following from the pharmacy: sal-ammonia, cinnamon, cloves, magnesium, camphor, bitters, licorice, gum arabic, theriac and vitriol.

Plants Used For Dyeing Textiles

The housewife and her daughter also searched the fields and woods for the plants that would yield dyes for her dye pots.

The first traces of dyeing woven material in Poland date back to the ancient Biskupin settlement. Remnants of dyeing plants such as *Galium vera* which dyed red and *Sambucus ebulus* and *Sambucus nigra* which dyed blue have been found. In diggings in Gdansk from the 12th and 13th century, the people were using *Polygonum aviculare* for dying blue, *Iris pseudacorus* for yellow. In the Gdansk diggings, it was determined that thread was being dyed as well as entire lengths of fabrics.

Many centuries later, the women of Poland were still using a variety of plants for dyeing fabrics. The growing of flax for linen and raising sheep for wool were very important cottage industries. Besides using cochineal and indigo, the country women produced a wide array of soft, durable dye colors from the following plants:

Alnus glutinosa—(alder tree) black from bark

Anthemis tinctoria—(golden marguerite) yellow from flowers

Betula alba—(birch) yellow from the leaves/green from the bark

Borago officinalis—(borage) blue from the leaves

Carthamus tinctorius—(safflower or false saffron) red

Fraxinus excelsior—(ash tree) yellow from the leaves

Galium verum—(ladies bedstraw) red from the root

Genista tinctoria—(broom, dyers weed) yellow from leaves/flowers

Hypericum perforatum—(St. John's wort) yellow from flowers

Lycopodium clavatum—(running ground pine) yellow

Origanum vulgare—(wild marjoram) shades of red from root

Quercus robur—(oak) black to light brown from bark

Rubia tinctorum—(madder) red from the roots

Salix alba—(willow) yellow/cinnamon from the bark

Urtica dioica—(nettle) green from the leaves

Verbascum Thapsus—(mullein) yellow/green from flower

Herbs drying near stove in country cottage.

Bee hive from Łowicz region.

Bees and Beehives

A bee skep or beehive was a standard feature in most Polish cottage gardens. Sugar, either from cane or from the sugar beet, was a luxury known only to the wealthy. For the Polish peasant, sweetness had to be obtained by other means, generally honey. Served on bread, it provided a simple meal. It also sweetened their tea, was used to make *pierniki* (a honey cookie that was made during Christmas and Easter), and of course, was used to make syrups for medicinal purposes—especially for coughs and colds. Honey was not only important for home use but it also could generate extra income. Those who managed to have more than enough for their own needs took their honey to market to sell. The making of mead and wax candles was also an important part of the rural economy, all of which drove the rural homeowner to set out some hives in his wife's garden.

The bee skeps ranged from the simple, old-fashioned dome shaped beehive made of wicker or straw to hollowed out logs. Others took on a variety of shapes and figures, often whittled or carved by the peasant himself who gave vent to his whimsical and creative urges.

If the year was a good one, the middle of July saw the first gathering of honey from the beehives. Sometimes it was gathered again in the latter part of September. Extracting the honey from the comb was a simple matter. The honeycombs were gathered in a bowl or pail and placed near a source of warmth such as the stove. Care had to be taken to make sure the stove was not too hot or it would melt the wax of the honey comb. Slowly, the honey would drip to the bottom of the pail. It was then stored in clay pots, bottles or wooden kegs made of linden or alder.

After the honey was removed, the wax comb was melted down by placing it in water and heating until the comb melted. Any debris in the wax was picked out with a spoon. Then it was strained through a cloth bag. The cooled wax was kept in a clean cloth in the attic or alcove. The wax was either donated to the church for molding into candles or kept for making candles for home use.

Bee Skeps, above, and old fashioned Bee Skep, below.

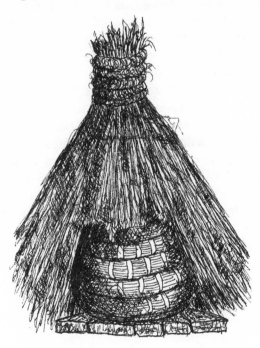

77

Bee Plants Used in Poland

Alfalfa	Heather	Mint
Angelica	Hyssop	Parsley
Basil	Lavender	Red Clover
Borage	Lemon Balm	Savory
Chamomile	Linden	Thyme
Coriander	Marjoram	
Dill		

Because they were simple and informal, actual garden plans of Polish peasant cottages from the past are, sadly, not available. What does exist, however, are individual personal memoirs, paintings and the writings of folklorists who took pains to document and preserve that which they saw. It is from these that we can reconstruct the cottage garden that existed in thousands of tiny hamlets and small villages throughout Poland. The most visual documents have been left to us by the Polish landscape painters of the latter half of the 19th century. Among these painters were Józef Chełmonski, Ferdynand Ruszczyc, Julian Fałat and Stanisław Masłowski. The latter painter lived chiefly in the small villages of Mazowsze while he worked. His son's memoirs recall the place where Masłowski lived and painted: "The cottage had a high veranda from which there is an excellent view of the garden and a beautiful, old apiary made of old stumps covered with primitive slats of wood. The cottage was modest but had on one side a typical garden filled with vegetables, sunflowers, dill, mallow and hollyhocks, along with a cherry tree and plum tree." The site became the inspiration for Masłowski's most famous painting called "Beehives in the Sun."

Bee Skep

Other Cottage Gardens

Kolbuszowa (Rzeszów)—1910

"There is a house, whitewashed with windows painted blue. On the window stand clay pots with a shiny glaze in which rosemary grows, smelling fragrantly from contact with the sun. In front of the house there is a garden. Against the rough timbers of the house are hollyhocks, standing as if on guard. Tucked near them, nodding in the sun, is larkspur whose leaves are slightly burnt. Inside there is a patch of nasturtiums perfuming the air. Close by is rue and mint. Near the fence is mallow, grown for use as an herb. Beyond the house a bit is a small orchard that contains a yellow pear that tastes best after the first frost.

First place, however, is taken by the apple tree whose skin can be peeled like thin paper. They become ripe on August 2."

Cracow Region—1871

"In front of the home there is a small garden planted with numerous flowers—peonies, pinks and chrysanthemums which are much loved by gardeners. There is also no small number of yellow lilies and white narcissus. Here are also found Blessed Mothers slippers (monkshood) and foxglove. No less important here is rosemary, hyssop, tarragon, mint and mugwort."

Kurpie Region (Mazowsze)- 1900's

"A window facing the street was decorated with curtains made from intricately cut paper to look like lace. On the windowsill are flowerpots filled with myrtle, scented rose geraniums and oleander. On the ground below sunning themselves against the house and enclosed by a wattle fence made of willow saplings are mugwort, mint and hyssop. There one can also see rue, lovingly tended by the unmarried girls of the house and comfrey, always of special concern to the Polish housewife."

Kurpie Region (Mazowsze)—1900's

"The garden was filled with flowers of various sizes and shapes—roses, tulips, peonies, lilies, dahlias, asters, and forget-me-nots, as well as chamomile and pot marigold.

Lublin Region—1940's

"Growing against the cottage were red, white and pink hollyhocks. Reaching practically to the eaves of the cottage, they looked like tall and graceful village girls. In one corner of the garden, so as not to produce too much shade, was a lilac tree. In some of the other gardens in the village a viburnum or mock orange was planted.

In the middle of the garden—putting on airs—was a rose bush. Against the fence, lilies. There wasn't an awful lot of room in the garden but in early spring there were primroses, narcissus and the much loved rose-colored bleeding heart. In the middle of summer there were pot marigold and the dark red tufts of wild millet. There were asters and gladioli and the large, double dahlias were considered a real prize in the garden. More frequently seen were the flat varieties in red and white colors."

Podhale—1890's

"In the Tatra regions of Poland there were numerous people who earned their living by climbing the mountains collecting shrubs, flowers and healing roots and herbs and then selling them to locals to use as medicine. They brought back larkspur, valerian and veronica. Angelica was used to incense the house and everyone in it against typhus. Eglantine was found in the mountain forests as was the elderberry. Monkshood, alpine sorrel and club moss were also collected."

Other Flowers Indigenous to Mountain Region

Lilium Martagon—turk's cap lily
Leontopodium alpinum—edelweiss
Carlina acaulis—carline thistle
Aster alpinis—alpine aster
Gentiana asclepiadea—gentian
Crocus scepusiensis—crocus
Primula elatior—oxlip

Łowicz—Warsaw Region

"The low and narrow windows here did not allow for many plants on the window sills but most of them have geranium and fuschia. More flowers were found in front of the home and were an extension of the house. In front of the house near the door there was always a bench in which the inhabitants could sit, take in the morning sun or evening air, greet passers-by and enjoy their garden. A lovely garden was the spirit

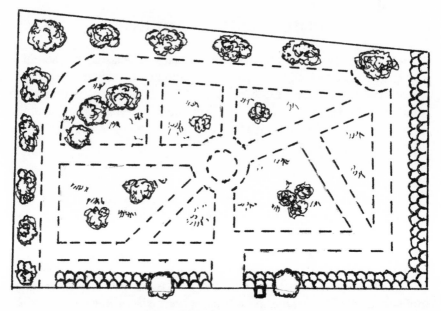

Herb garden in Łowicz region.

of the housewife. A poorly tended garden was a reflection on the housewife and her daughters. In the garden here we would find hollyhocks growing in the sun against the timbers of the house. There would be pinks, yellow and blue-purple lilies, mignonette, rue, mint, lovage, and myrtle."

Another Cottage Garden Dated 1890
"Near the house there is a small garden planted with beans, periwinkle, mulberry, peppermint, southernwood, soapwort and dahlia. Futher along we see an orchard with plum and sweet and sour cherry trees."

Folk Museum Garden
The above plan for an herb garden comes from the open air folk museum in Łowicz outside of Warsaw. It contains decorative and medicinal plants as well as beehives.

POLISH GARDENS OF THE PAST

List of plants in this herb garden include:

plantain	burdock	yellow loosestrife
elderberry	lovage	chamomile
meadow geranium	thyme	flaxseed
violet	peppermint	mallow
boxwood	marigold	centaury
beet	gentian	fools parsley
cornflower	shield fern	jimson weed
mullein	coltsfoot	heather
St. John's wort	wormwood	comfrey
yarrow	nettle	onion
horsetail	rue	
linden tree		

Kurpie Country Cottage Window

Window Gardens

And in the windows fragrant flowers were set,
Geranium, gillyflower and violet.
—Pan Tadeusz

To travel through the Polish countryside today and look at the homes is to see as Adam Mickiewicz did back in the 19th century. There is an almost universal tendency to have white lace curtains on the windows with geraniums, violets or a favorite houseplant on the windowsills.

Most Polish cottages were built of logs, some of which were very thick. When the windows were framed, it made for very deep windowsills. At the same time, however, the windows themselves were generally small, limiting the available light within the house. Subsequently, the country housewife placed only a small curtain across the top of the window to maximize light entering the house. If she could not afford real cloth curtains but was handy with paper and scissors, she fashioned herself a paper curtain. On the windowsill she placed pots of flowers and plants that could not survive the winter outdoors. Clay pots, either plain or glazed, contained rose geraniums, rosemary, an aloe plant or a pot of parsley or tarragon.

Another very important indoor windowsill plant was myrtle (*myrtus communis*) a small shrubby plant not to be confused with the trailing groundcover myrtle. It was during the reign of Zygmunt I and his Italian wife Bona Sforza that myrtle appeared in Poland. Like rosemary, this plant has a rich history in Polish wedding traditions, similar to that of northern and eastern Europe. Many old Polish photographs show a bride with sprigs of myrtle on the hemline of her dress and in the wreath on her head.

Plants Associated with Jesus Christ and Blessed Virgin Mary

Asplenium trichomanes (maidenhair fern)—Blessed Mother's hair

Artemisia abrotanum (southernwood)—Blessed Mother's tree

Briza media (quaking grass)—Blessed Mother's tears

Eriphorum vaginatum (cottongrass)—Lord Jesus's hair

POLISH HERBS, FLOWERS & FOLK MEDICINE

Gnaphalium sylvaticum (cudweed)—rye of Lord Jesus

Hypericum perforatum (St. John's wort)—bells of the Virgin Mary

Linaria vulgaris (butter and eggs, wild snapdragon)—flax of the Virgin Mary

Lysimachia vulgaris (yellow loosestrife)—pears of the Blessed Mother

Onopordon acanthium (cotton thistle)—Blessed Mother's thistle

Pulicaria dysenterica (fleabane)—herb of Jesus Christ

Sanquisorba officinalis (great burnet)- lambs of the Blessed Virgin

Trifolium repens (white clover)—hair of the blessed Virgin

Trigonella foenum graecum (fenugreek)—God's grass

Verbascum thapsus (mullein)—braids of the Blessed Virgin

Verbena officinalis (vervain)—baskets of the Blessed Virgin

CHAPTER IV

Herbs and Flowers

The following plants are listed according to the names commonly used. The botanical name follows for accurate identification. I have made every possible effort to maintain accuracy and used numerous references to check and recheck in order to accurately interpret the Polish names of certain plants. I have also tried to include folk names where possible. The recipes are all from old Polish herbals and cookbooks.

Alder, European
Alnus glutinosa
Olcha

"The meadows were veiled in a low creeping haze, through which tufts of alders peered out like puffs of dark smoke."
—*The Peasants: Spring*

In the Rzeszów region in southeastern Poland, the alder can be found growing abundantly near rivers and streams and is easily identified by its red bark. According to legend, at the time of Creation, there was a rivalry between God and the devil. The wolf was shaped by God but the devil tried to intervene and bring it to life. However, the wolf refused to breathe and live. It was only when infused with the power of God that the wolf sprang to life and began to attack the devil. The devil hid in an alder tree but the wolf caught hold of his heal and blood ran down the trunk. From that time forward, the alder has had its reddish bark.

Medicinally, a decoction of the fresh leaves was used to treat wounds that had difficulty healing. Such a mixture was also used to make a poultice and applied to breasts that were hardened and engorged.

Angelica

Angelica
Archangelica angelica
Arcydzięgiel litwor, Ziela Ducha Świętego

According to archeological diggings, angelica was known in Poland 2500 years ago. It was also found in old Polish monasteries of the 12th century and called the Herb of the Holy Ghost.

Angelica grows wild in the northwest regions of Poland and along the Carpathian Tatras and Pieniny mountains. Early herbals recommend that it "be planted in the garden against a fence where it's less likely to be damaged."

According to Syrenius, "the powder of this root will free the chest and lungs of fluid and also be of service to those heavy in childbearing; a syrup of the root boiled in wine or honey will draw out any poisons or venom." He also suggested: "In the event of some kind of troublesome misfortune, gather the root with care during the descent of the lion's cub and hang it around your neck. It will drive away cares and cause a merry heart." An infusion of the root of this herb was also used as protection against cholera.

According to Father Kneipp, a tea made from the root of angelica effectively eliminated a hangover, a runny nose and any inflammation of the lungs and bronchus. A decoction of angelica root, added to vinegar, served as a linement for gout, rheumatism, pains of the spine and general weakness. The root or dried leaves were used as a treatment for epilepsy and as a gargle for scarlet fever.

REMEDY FOR CHRONIC CONSTIPATION

1/2 c. angelica root
1/2 c. arnica root
1 qt. white wine

Mix together 1/2 c. angelica root and 1/4 c. arnica root in 1 quart white wine and allow to soften for a week. Boil and strain. Drink a full whiskey glass of the liquid before eating.

An herb liquor called Benedictine originated with the Benedictine monks. The creator was Bernard Vincelli (born in 1510) and originally carried the name D.O.M. Benedictine, the DOM standing for Deo Optimo Maximo or For the Glory of God.

Lucyna Cwierczakiewicz (1829-1901) wrote one of the most popular and practical cookbooks for the Polish housewife called *Only Practical Recipes*. She offered this recipe.

HOMEMADE BENEDICTINE

1 tsp. root of angelica	3 small, green bitter oranges
1 Tbsp. root of calamus	1/2 tsp. aloe
1 Tbsp. myrrh	1 stick vanilla
1 Tbsp. cinnamon	1/8 tsp. nutmeg
2 Tbsp. orange peel	1/8 tsp. saffron
1/8 tsp. ginger	4 cloves

Soak everything in a half of a quart of the finest spirytus for three days and no longer. Strain. Make a syrup from 5 lbs. of sugar using a quart of boiling water per pound and add to alcohol mixture. Pour into bottles and cork.

Anise
Pimpinella anisum
Biedrzeniec anyż

This herb was brought to Poland by the Benedictine monks and grown in the monastery gardens as well as the gardens of Kazimierz the Great (1310-1370). Syreniusz noted not only that "here in our more delightful gardens, it begins to be seen more frequently" but also that there were two types of anise: one was helpful for women, the other for men. In later centuries it was grown and exported in large quantities in the region of Pinczow.

In folk medicine, anise was used for stomach ailments, mainly for distention. It also reduced temperatures, acted as a diuretic, expectorant and even anti-asthmatic. Mixed with lard and swallow wort (*vicentoxicum*) it served as a salve for lice and nits.

The oil of anise was rubbed on the body to repel troublesome insects, especially mosquitos. In ancient times it served to flavor liquor, to improve the taste of medicine and was an additive to dishes difficult to digest.

Beet
Beta vulgaris
Burak

Among the best oil paintings of Polish painter Leon Wyczółkowski (1852-1936) were fields of beets and peasants digging beets. He once said to his students: "If you want to learn to mix paints, please sit with your palette before a field of red beets. Then you will learn just what your abilities are."

Medicinally, beets were used to treat sore throats and colds. The beet was grated, steeped in hot water and drained through a colander. A teaspoonful of vinegar and a spoonful of honey were added to the juice and used as a gargling agent. It was reputed to cure the swelling within the hour. In some districts of Poland, the juice from cooked beets was boiled with sage and also used for sore throats. The warm juice was dropped into the ear if someone suffered from buzzing in the ears. The leaves of the beet applied to the head soothed headaches.

Beets and beet soup have been a staple of Polish cuisine for centuries among both peasants and nobility. Beets mixed with horseradish, called *ćwikła,* was a standard condiment for meat dishes (especially pork) and frequently found on the table at Easter time to accompany sausage and ham.

Basil, Sweet
Ocimum basilicum
Bazylia pospolita

In the 16th century, Syrenius recalled that this plant "is sown indoors in pots for a perfume." It was supposed to "remove a runny nose just from its fragrance" and "help when one has trouble passing water and bring dreams to those who have trouble sleeping."

Belladonna
Atropa belladonna
Pokrzyk, wilka jagoda

Found in the Carpathian regions of Poland, the berries of this plant are poisonous and one of the chief reasons it has always been associated in Polish folklore with witches and evil.

Bellflower
Campanula trachelium
Dzwonek

For pains in the ear, the blossoms of bellflower were gathered, boiled in a covered pan and after steeping the liquid, used to wash the ears. If one had pain in the stomach, the root of this plant was cooked and spirytus added. After steeping for three hours, a small drink helped ease the pain. In the smaller villages, children suffering from consumption were bathed in this herb: if the child's skin darkened after such a bath, it was a sign that he/she would live. If it didn't, the disease would surely take him/her.

Birch
Betula pendula
Brzoza, brzezina

"Meanwhile the old men went on drinking mead
And passed the birch-bark snuff box to and fro"
—*Pan Tadeusz*

Birch was used by the Slavs as a harbinger of Spring and as a symbol of eternity. It protected against witchcraft and the evil eye, bringing people good fortune and happiness. During the religious customs of Pentecost and Corpus Christi branches of birch were used to decorate the house and altars. The tree was also used for making baskets and brooms. Cattle driven out to the fields for the first time in spring were driven out with birch branches, in the belief that the cows would give as much milk as the birch had given sap. In some Slav tribes, the first writings were completed on the interior of the birch bark. In Poznan, it was believed that the souls of dead girls, called willies, walked among the birches and that in February and March they danced in the light of the moon for the death of any person who found him/herself among them.

Medicinally, the birch had multiple uses from the catkins, leaves, bark, and syrup. It was used externally to treat joint problems, bedsores, burns and scrapes by using compresses and salves. The young budding birch leaves, soaked in spirytus, helped stop bleeding wounds. It was also used as an infusion by pouring spirytus on the catkins and taken internally for rheumatism and colds.

The sap obtained from the birch tree was called *oskoła*. It was valued as a drink that cleansed the blood and improved hair growth. This syrup was also called *brzozownik* and considered a "drink divine" which maintained strength, beauty and firm flesh. It was gathered from ten-year old trees and drawn from the south side of the trunk. Alcohol mixed with the sap of birch helped prevent oily, thinning or limp hair. When fermented, the sap made a tasty wine and a healthy vinegar.

The tar from birch bark was used as both an external and internal treatment against lice, worms and ticks in humans and animals. Boiled in water, the bark was an effective remedy for a fever.

The soot from birch was used to make a dark printer's ink. The leaves boiled with alum and chalk would yield a yellow shade which was used to color paper, fabric or Easter eggs called *pisanki*. A bath made from the infusion of the leaves was helpful for cleaning and regenerating the skin and the removal of blemishes and blotches.

BIRCH BATH

1 c. birch leaves
1 qt. water

Boil together the birch leaves with the quart of water. Allow to stand for 20 minutes. Strain. Add to bath water.

Blueberry
Vaccinium myrtillus
Borówka czarna

One of the oldest medicines in northern Europe, blueberry grows wild all over Poland in highlands, lowlands, pine forests and mountain clearings. Because they grew well in wet, acidic soil, blueberries were exported in large quantities from Poland for the production of alcohol in the 19th century.

Kneipp recommended 10-12 drops of *borowiak* on sugar for stomach pain. *Borowiak* was a drink made from blueberry and vodka. Fresh, or cooked and forced through a sieve, blueberry was useful as a poultice for eczema, spots or burns and also wounds (after first washing the wound with whey). Raw blueberries can cause diarrhea but the dried and cooked berries are an effective remedy against it.

At one time blueberry was used to color hides or skins. Along with alum, it was used to dye wool for a blue pigment. In the kitchen blueberry was used to make syrups, marmalades, pierogies and soups.

HERBS AND FLOWERS

BLUEBERRY SOUP

1 c. fresh blueberries
3 c. water
4 Tbsp. heavy cream
1 Tbsp. potato flour

Cook the fresh berries in the water. Press through a sieve. Mix the cream with the potato flour and add to the strained berries. Cook and sweeten to taste. Allow to cool. Serve chilled.

Borage
Borago officinalis
Ogórecznik lekarski

In ancient times this plant was called *miodnik* (honey plant) to indicate its usefulness for attracting bees in the garden. Marcin of Urzędow wrote: "Anyone who knows herbs, knows borage." It was used in his time to cleanse the blood. In old Poland it was also added to wine to "strengthen the heart and to promote good thoughts," as well as to relieve an afflicted stomach, decrease fevers and colds, assist in chest and lung ailments and even be an effective remedy against consumption.

Cooked with chicken soup it was a helpful treatment for jaundice. The root, boiled in water, was helpful in banishing nausea, hot coppers and a dry throat. Eaten with butter and almonds, it acted as a cleansing agent.

In the kitchen, the leaves and flowers were added to all spring salads creating a cucumber taste, hence its Polish name of cucumber. It can be added to soup such as Ukrainian barszcz, hot chicken soup or cold soups. Liquers, syrups and juices were made from it. The fresh flowers were fried in syrup and ground with sugar. The leaves also yielded a blue dye. A decoction of borage was helpful for boils, pimples, first-degree burns or scrapes of the epidermis.

BORAGE WASH

1/2 to 1 c. borage leaves
1 qt. water

Boil together the borage with the water for 5 minutes and allow to stand for another 15 minutes. Apply to affected areas.

Boxwood
Buxus sempiverens
Bukspan ogrodowy

Boxwood was one of the chief plants used in Polish gardening for knot gardens and edgings in formal herb gardens. Sprigs of boxwood were tucked into Easter baskets when they were taken to church to be blessed on Holy Saturday. It was also used to decorate the food on Easter Sunday, tucked in-between coils of sausage or around a ham.

The leaves of boxwood, soaked in alcohol and applied to the head helped severe headaches.

Bryony, white
Bryonia alba
Przestęp pospolity

The leaves of this plant are supposed to resemble a child, (possessing a head, ears, eyes and stomach). The Polish people feared digging for this herb, believing that whomever dug out this herb would be destroying his/her happiness. If found on personal property the owner often fenced it in. The leaves and stems could be removed, however, and used for a variety of spells and medication. Witches kept this plant hidden on their person. For them it grew anywhere—even a pot without dirt! The cooked root was effective in healing any wounds on a horse's hoof.

Burdock
Arctium lappa
Łopian

About burdock, Syreniusz wrote: "The mashed root applied to pain recedes." He also suggested: "For a bite by a rabid dog, the grated root mixed with salt should be applied...for burns from fire or sun—grate the leaves, mix with egg whites and apply." The root of burdock mixed with beef fat made a healing salve.

Besides the root, the leaves and seeds of burdock were equally useful in Polish folk medicine. It was an old treatment for cleansing the blood, treating gout, rheumatism, skin disorders and hemorrhoids. The leaves were frequently used for burns, festering wounds and the fresh juice used to wash greasy skin.

SKIN CLEANSER

1/4 c. burdock root
1/4 c. dried nettle leaves
1/4 c. dried horsetail

Boil for 15 minutes in 3 c. water. Strain. Add to bath water.
For greasy hair, use the following to make a rinse after washing:

HAIR RINSE

1/2 c. burdock root
3/4 Tbsp. horsetail leaf
3/4 Tbsp. chamomile
1/2 c. soapwort
1 Tbsp. nettle

Make a dry mixture of the above ingredients. Throw 1 Tbsp. of the herb mixture onto a cup of boiling water and boil for a few minutes. Allow to cool. Strain and use to rinse hair.

Burnet saxifrage
Pimpinella saxifraga
Biedrzeniec

The leaves and root of saxifrage were steeped in spirytus and felt to be useful against cholera, dysentery and other abdominal discomforts. From this usefulness in diseases which cause mass epidemics, such as dysentery and cholera, there arose a Polish folk tale. It was said that at one time there were three women who were responsible for death; they wiped people out by the thousands. One time, one of these three was injured and became lame. She could not walk as quickly and therefore had trouble keeping up with the others. When the other two picked up their pace and left her behind she called out to them to have mercy and walk more slowly. When her plea fell on deaf ears, she threatened that she would give the people an effective remedy against them. This brought no response. Becoming very angry she fulfilled her threat. Going through each village, she called out "People, people, eat and drink saxifrage and you will be safe from death." The people took her suggestion seriously and the hand of death was stayed. The other two women became very angry at what she had done and threw themselves in fury upon her. The lame one protected herself with the long scythe and one of the women, falling upon it, was killed. The second fell on the scythe of her dying sister and she, too, was killed. Now only one woman seeks people and there is no medicine to protect against her.

Cabbage
Brassica oleracea
Kapusta

"A cabbage sits and bows her scrawny pate
Musing about her vegetable fate"
—*Pan Tadeusz*

A popular food staple throughout all of Poland, cabbage was also a standby for treating common ailments. Fresh cabbage leaves were applied to the head for headaches. Sauerkraut was applied to swollen areas to help reduce swelling.

Campion
Lychnis coronaria
Firletka

According to Syreniusz, in the times before Polish people had access to cotton, the dry leaf of campion was used as a candle wick and gave it its second name: *knotka* (knot). It was also known as the Little Rose of the Blessed Mother.

Caraway
Carum carvi
Kminek zwyczajny

In the Middle Ages, caraway was a trade item found in parts of Belgium and Poland, however, it was already being used as a spice from the time of the first Piasts. It was added to beet soup and all varieties of meats and baked goods, especially breads. In olden days it was also used as a medication for stomach ailments, cramps, liver problems and as a diuretic. It was usually ingested in the form of crushed seeds or mixed with wine or vodka. An infusion of the seeds was used as an enema to treat diarrhea and dysentery. Its highest healing powers were granted when collected on June 24.

Caraway expels gas when mixed with anise, coriander and fennel. These three seeds were assumed to have magical strength and were carried in bags hung around the neck. If a child was thought to be "troubled by demons," a pan of boiling caraway and water was placed under the cradle. It was noted that a person would be free from mosquitos if "on going to sleep will chew on caraway and spread the chewed mass on their hands and face."

Very often found growing in the wild, caraway was used extensively in meat dishes especially pork, cabbage and potato dishes and also in cheeses, soups and sauces.

APPETITE STIMULANT

1 Tbsp. crushed caraway seeds
1 c. boiling water

Pour boiling water over the crushed caraway seeds. Allow to
stand for 15 minutes. Drink a half a glass three times a day.

Carrot, Wild
Daucus carota
Marchew zwyczajna

The grated root of wild carrot was applied to burns, ulcerated and/or
inflamed areas, or to draw out pus.

Cattail, Common
Typha latifolia
Rogoża szerokolista

The fluff from the cattail was applied to burnt areas of the body to
promote healing.

Celandine
Chelidonium majus
Jaskółcze ziele, glistnik

Celandine is one of the many plants depicted in one of the finest
masterpieces of European late-medieval carving and the most
magnificent piece of art in Poland—the Marian altar at St. Mary's
Church in Cracow. From the historic work of artist Wit Stwosz (1477-
1533), the altar has become a source of information about plants
growing in and around Cracow during that era. The altar, a pentaptych,
is populated by two hundred figures with scenes from the church placed
in realistic interiors and landscapes. Looking at the altar one can learn
about the inhabitants of the old city of Cracow—how the different classes

dressed, what kind of arms they used, what diseases they suffered from and what kind of plants were growing near the city. The plants shown in large or small groups appear predominantly in the outer bas-relief panels. Violets are seen in Adoration of the Magii; Three Mary's in the Garden shows dandelion; The Resurrection depicts dandelion, plantain, and violet. Appearing in other panels are wild strawberry, twayblade, thistle and early spring plants such as ferns, clover and silverweed. Most of the plants are depicted in the last panel of Christ as Gardener. Christ is depicted with a spade in hand surrounded by lily-of-the-valley, dead nettle and celandine.

Celandine is found growing wild all over Poland. The stem and leaves yield a yellowish-orange sap used to treat warts and pustules. The sap was applied over a period of a few days to weeks until the warts or pustules disappeared.

Centaury
Centaurium Erythraea
Tysiącznik

The gypsies of Poland made a tea of the leaves when experiencing a lack of appetite, gall bladder and liver problems. For abdominal pains, for colds and for increasing appetite, a decoction was made of the root. Another method involved making a drink by soaking the flowers in whiskey or vodka.

Chamomile
Matricaria chamomilla
Rumianek pospolity, maruna

In the 15th century an oil was already being extracted from chamomile in Poland to serve as medication. Herbalist Stefan Falimirz recommended that the juice of chamomile be mixed with vodka to heal the liver and increase urination. He also noted that "the flower of chamomile causes headache and eye-strain to decrease. Wormwood and chamomile aid an easy delivery." The yellow flower, dried, crumbled and mixed with honey in a tea relieved colds and muscle spasms. Steeped in water or boiled in beer, it increased appetite, and strengthened the chest. Polish mothers gave colicky babies a tea made from chamomile. It was also used to freshen old meat and to lighten hair.

SOOTHING CHAMOMILE BATH

1 1/2 c. chamomile flowers
1 qt. water

Bring to a boil. Strain and add to bath water.

Chicory
Cichorium intybus
Cykoria podróżnik

The roots were steeped in spirytus together with the leaves and roots of anise against cholera and other abdominal pain. The mountain people used the roots to bathe consumptive children.

Coltsfoot
Tussilago farfara
Podbiał pospolity

Coltsfoot was a plant that had a wide range of uses and was prepared in a variety of ways. The flowers and leaves, mixed with other herbs, were used chiefly for a dry cough and hoarseness. Men dried the leaves, crumbled them and mixed them with tobacco for coughs and lung troubles. The smoke of the dried burning leaves was used to incense an ill person suffering from asthma. Fresh, crushed leaves were mixed with honey and applied to any swelling.

Young, fresh leaves were also applied to abcesses with thick roots. A decoction of the leaves was used to wash wounds and for compresses to apply over tumors. A tea from the leaves "thins phlegm." A home syrup could also be made by covering the flowers and leaves with sugar.

REMEDY FOR HOARSENESS

1 tsp. dried coltsfoot
1 tsp. dried marshmallow
1 c. boiling water

Pour boiling water into cup containing the coltsfoot and marshmallow. Allow to steep. Drink 2—3 glasses a day.

Comfrey
Symphytum officinalae
Żywokost

Comfrey is instantly recognized by many second and third generation Polish-Americans as a plant found in their mother's and grandmother's gardens. The most frequently cited use was that of healing broken bones and taking away the aches of arthritis and rheumatism. First generation Polish immigrant women have given me numerous recipes for its use. Most common was steeping the leaves and/or mashed up root in rubbing alcohol for a few weeks, straining and using as a linement on aching parts. Another individual with severe stomach and intestinal difficulties steeped the leaves in whiskey for a few weeks and then drank a shot glass twice a day until he recovered.

Old Polish herbals do suggest that after breaking any body part, it helps to apply comfrey by making a poultice of the fresh leaves or the broken part washed in a decoction made of the root or leaves. Another much preferred method was to make a salve from the root by grating or cutting it into small, thin pieces and adding to unsalted butter. This was melted over a slow heat until it began to darken. The mixture was strained, allowed to cool and then applied to broken areas. A more direct method was to dig out the root, mash it and apply it to broken bones.

If there was no immediate need for the root, it was dug out at the end of summer, washed carefully and any darkened or rotted areas cut away. It was then allowed to thoroughly dry. The dried, powdered root helped stop nosebleeds when inhaled like snuff or placed into the nose with cotton.

A tea was also made from the leaves to improve digestion.

Cornflower
Centaurea cyanus
Chaber, bławatek, modrak

"The maid for Telimena twisted now
A plait of cornflowers, which with fingers deft
She pinned on Zosia's head from right to left
The flowers against her pale gold tresses worn
Stood out as lovely as on ears of corn."
—*Pan Tadeusz*

This is an ancient plant which originated in the southwest regions of Poland and grows wild among the wheat and rye. The powdered root was known to stem the flow of blood from the nose and wounds. It was used to heal cuts and boils that would arise from shaving by sprinkling the powder of the flower. For the eyes, a mixture was made of vodka and vinegar from the flower in June. Old herbals recommended it for "inflammation of the liver, poisonous bites, rotting gums" and also

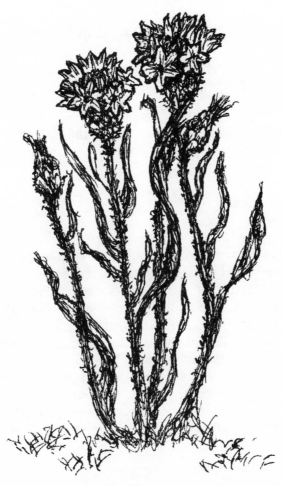

Cornflower

against "pestilential air."

Juice from the petals of bluebottle was used for a very long time to obtain a blue dye for dyeing wool and making paints. The dry flower was also an additive to making incense. An infusion of the flower served to rid the hair of dandruff. A decoction of this herb was sometimes added to bathwater to ease the pangs of gout. Along with eyebright, it was used for conjunctivitis.

EYEWASH

1 Tbsp. dried cornflower
1 c. boiling water

Pour boiling water over the dried cornflower. Steep for 15 minutes. Strain. Use as an eyewash.

Coriander
Coriandrum sativum
Kolendra siewna

Coriander was known in Poland during the time of the first Piasts (960 A.D.). In the Middle Ages it was valued both as a spice and as medication. Marcin of Urzędow wrote: "Everyone knows of coriander—even children in diapers know of the sugared coriander." It was helpful for hangovers, headaches, stomach aches, diarrhea and bad tastes in the mouth. The oil obtained through distillation was known "to move gas and strengthen the stomach."

In the kitchen, coriander was added to pickled meat, to marinate vegetables such as cabbage, pickles, beets and mushrooms as well as flavoring for vinegar. Old recipes suggest washing clothes and linens in coriander to sweeten the smell of perspiration as well as to exterminate insects.

Couch Grass
Agropyron repens
Pyrz

During times of famine, couch grass was a very popular substitute and or/filler in baking bread. It was washed, dried and crumbled. It was ground with wheat and oat grains in the home quern and used in baking bread or making pancakes. It was believed to give added strength.

Cranberry
Vaccinum vitus-idea
Borówka brusznica

Cranberries can be found growing wild in Poland. They were used to treat the aches of rheumatism. The berries cooked in sugar were ingested for stomach troubles, diarrhea and to stimulate appetite. A decoction of the leaves was used as a diuretic for renal stones; the crushed berries were applied to burns.

Cumin, Black
Nigella sativa
Czarnuszka siewna

Marcin of Urzędow recalls: "People are very familiar with black cumin because they eat bread with it and it is very tasty and healthy." Drunk with wine at night, Syreniuz claimed cumin "decreases phlegm from the lungs and increases milk in a mother's breast." It was effective in expelling worms and a useful remedy against snake bites. In the summer, teamed-up with wormwood, it repelled mosquitos. The oil extracted from the seeds and mixed with vinegar helped eliminate freckles.

Dahlia
Dahlia
Georginia

The single and collerette-type dahlias were much more common in cottage gardens than the larger, giant varieties. A writer, reminiscing about growing up in a small village in the Lublin region, depicted this particular custom from his formative years in the 1940's: "On Sunday people from the surrounding villages came to our village for Mass since it had the only church for miles around. Men, women and children walked barefoot most of the way and paused only as they approached the

107

village to put on their boots and shoes which they had carried with them to save on wear and tear. All of the bachelors that came to church brought with them one flower—a dark dahlia. In front of the church they met their sweethearts and gave them the flower. The girls made a bouquet of the dahlias and placed it on the church altar."

Daisy
Bellis perennis
Stokroć margarytka

Among the peasant and nobility, it was the custom to tear off daisy petals in order to predict whether someone was loved. The Polish version:

Kocha	Loves me
Nie kocha	Loves me not
Serdecznie	Sincerely
Statecznie	Sedately
Bardzo mało	Very little
Wcale nie	Not at all

An infusion of the flower was drunk in the morning and at night for a fever. It was also very helpful for a cough and consumption.

Dandelion
Taraxacum officinale
Mniszek pospolity

"There were clumps of vetches without end, buttercups and dandelions innumerable, and the purple flowers of the thistle and clover, and daisies with chamomiles—and countless others..."
—*The Peasants: Summer*

In the 16th century, the dandelion became a very versatile herb used in the removal of freckles and liver spots, fevers, contagious diseases, liver and stomach ailments and even the three-day malaria. Cooked with lentils, it was administered for diarrhea and dysentery. The root, boiled with wine or vinegar, was given in situations where there was difficulty voiding. As a treatment for the liver it was prepared in conjunction with fennel. It was best collected in May along with the root. Tinctures were made with wine or vodka. The fresh leaf was applied to cuts and stab wounds. Even to this very day, a syrup is made from the flower and used for coughs.

DANDELION BATH
(for eczema)

1 tbsp. burdock root
1 tbsp. dandelion root
1 qt. water

Boil together the root burdock, dandelion root and water. Strain. Drink one-half glass 2 to 3 times a day. Also add to bath water.

DANDELION SYRUP

400 fresh dandelion flowers
1 qt. cold water
2 lbs. sugar
1 lemon

Place the fresh dandelion flowers in the cold water. Boil together for one hour, covered. Strain through a fine gauze and add sugar, the juice of one lemon and cook together another 2 hours under mild heat. Pour into bottles and seal immediately. Used for coughs and the beginnings of colds.

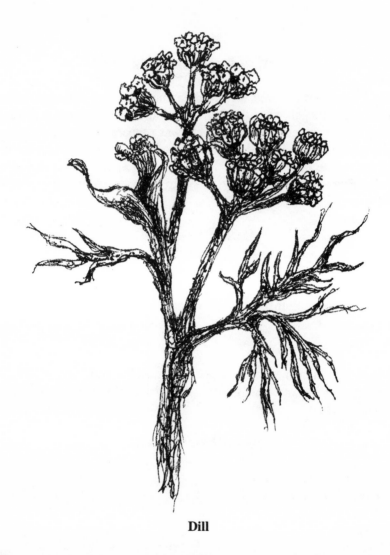

Dill

Dill
Anethum graveolens
Koper ogrodowy

In the Łowicz region, dill was helpful in treating pain in the eyes. The seeds of dill were soaked in water, strained and the water used to wash or rinse the eyes. Marcin of Urzędow indicated that garden dill was "very good for treating nightmares."

HERBS AND FLOWERS

Dill was even more important in Polish cuisine. As early as the 17th century, Syreniusz indicated that "dill is useful not only as a medicine but also used at the table...the leaves are used in meats, soups and vegetables...the seed is also added to pickling cabbage, salting meat and added to sausages for stuffing." He recommended using the entire plant when making pickles—the root, stem, leaves and seeds.

Dill is still used generously in Polish cuisine today especially for hors d'oeuvres, salads, soups and sauces. Sown early in spring, the feathery leaves are available by the end of May and can be used throughout the summer to enhance numerous dishes. Polish cooks have traditionally preserved the feathery foliage of dill for winter use by chopping it very fine and packing it between layers of salt in stone crocks or jars and storing in a cool place.

Cucumbers With Sour Cream

2 cucumbers, peeled and sliced very thinly
1/2 c. sour cream
1/2 tsp. salt
1-2 Tbsp. vinegar
1 tsp. dillweed

Sprinkle salt over sliced cucumbers and allow to stand for 10-15 minutes. Drain out excess water. Add sour cream and vinegar to cucumbers. Sprinkle with dill weed. Serve chilled as salad.

Edelweiss
Leontopodium alpinum
Szarotka

Found growing in the valleys and mountain pastures of the Tatra mountains, edelweiss is a very popular motif in the folk art of the mountain people. It is currently on the endangered flora list.

Eyebright
Euphrasia officinalis
Świetlik łąkowy

Eyebright was not recognized in Poland until the Middle Ages. In old herbals it was said to reduce dryness and burning of the eyes and correct poor eyesight. The herb was dried and crushed to a fine powder, dissolved in water and used as an eyewash that was effective in both animals as well as humans. Sometimes the fresh flower was rubbed with sugar and placed in the sun. The resulting syrup was ingested and supposed to strengthen the eyes.

Elderberry
Sambucus nigra
Dziki bez czarny

A common plant throughout all of Europe, elderberry was also called *bez lekarski* in Poland, i.e., medicinal elderberry to indicate its properties. The flower, fruit, leaves, bark and even the seed of this plant were utilized. From the flowers, pillows were made which were heated and used as a treatment for earache, stomachache and the pains of rheumatism. Fruit syrups, jams, and wine were made from the berries, all having health-giving properties. The young shoots were used as a salve for rheumatism. The new leaves and shoots were dried and ground to a powder and then added to chicken soup or milk soup as an aid for obstructions. Father Kneipp suggested that all who have a sedentary life should consider drinking 1 Tbsp. of elderberry jam in a glass of boiling water to clear the kidneys and stomach each day.

Elderberry was also used to treat skin abrasions and pulled tendons on horses. A liniment made from a handful of elderberry flowers and a handful of curly mint steeped in wine and cooked to a paste was applied to warm the pulled tendon.

It had magical as well as medicinal uses. If the white blossoming flowers were cut and used on the night of June 24 (St. John's Eve), they were felt to be more effective. Syreniusz stated "for bites from lizards, the boiled root should be drunk and the wound washed. For women, the juice of the berry will color the hair black." For headaches, the flowers were soaked in alcohol and applied to the head as a compress.

Useful in Polish kitchens from time immemorial, housewives made soups, syrups, marmalades, preserves, jams, gelatins, teas and wine.

ELDERBERRY SYRUP

30 clusters of berries, cleaned and separated
2 lbs. sugar
1 qt. of water

Cook sugar and water and add a little lemon juice to taste. Pour onto the berries and cook briefly. Allow to stand for 12 hours. Pour syrup into bottles and jars.

Elecampane
Inula Helenium
Omian, dziewosił

This plant was useful as a medication for impetigo in people and cows and horses. The root, grated into a fat of some kind, helped scabby, itchy or acned areas.

Flax
Linum usitatissimum
Len zwyczajny

"...and a few plots of flax in the hollows gleamed blue with delicate flowers—childlike eyes that seemed blinking in the glare."
—*The Peasants: Summer*

Originally from the southeast, there are seven varieties of flax in Poland. Syreniusz recommended it for healing blotches and blemishes, herpes, scabs and even rough fingernails. Flax was also an effective remedy for an old cough and hoarseness. At the onset of a cold filaments of flax were burned, and the smoke was inhaled a few times a day. The seeds were chewed for help with intestinal pain.

Gypsies used it for all stomach ailments by ingesting the seeds and drinking them with hot water. Flax seeds were a trusted remedy among Polish immigrants for constipation.

FLAX SEED FACIAL

Crush 2 tsp. flax seeds and cover with boiling water. When cooled, apply the mash to the face, avoiding the areas close to the eyes. After 20 minutes remove carefully.

Fennel
Foeniculum vulgare
Koper włoski

In the Middle Ages, fennel was grown in the monastery gardens and on the estates of Kazimierz the Great (1333-1370). There were over 200 recipes for its use, including that of an aphrodisiac.

The Slavic name for fennel—*koper*—is derived from the word *kopeć* which indicated aroma. In old Poland it was used both as a culinary herb and as a medicinal one. Marcin of Urzędow wrote: "fennel is known by everyone in Italy. They use it in baked cakes and bread."

It was believed that its root, boiled in vinegar, would remove any rash or pimples due to fever and that a half tablespoon of the ashes of the burnt herb taken every morning and evening would relieve dizziness. The burnt root was also supposed to "open the glands and strengthen sweat." An infusion made of the powdered seeds was used to wash the eyes for any sores and rubbed into the scalp to encourage growth. The seeds also relieved colds of the stomach, regulated menstruation and acted as a diuretic.

Fennel was taken to church to be blessed on The Feast of Corpus Christi.

Foxglove
Digitalis purpurea
Naparstnik

The Polish name for foxglove is the English equivalent of "thimble" and it can be seen growing in many cottage gardens throughout Poland. Herbals mention the fact that it became more widespread in Polish gardens after Englishman William Withering had made his careful studies of the properties of the plant in the 18th century. Housewives "save the dried leaves and flowers in little cloth bags." It was known to strengthen the heart and rid the body of excess fluids.

Garlic
Allium sativum
Czosnek

In his herbal, Syreniusz listed almost one hundred medicinal uses for garlic including: increasing urination, opening the veins of the liver and giving aid to asthmatics. In small village life, water in which garlic had been soaking helped horses with a cough. It was also believed to have mysterious powers. Hung over a door, it drove away illnesses and enemies as testified in this old Polish proverb: *Ucieka jak czarownica od czosnku*, translated, "runs like a witch from garlic."

Gentian, marsh
Gentiana pneumonanthe
Goryczka wąskolistna

Folk names for this plant were *rękawki Matki Boskiej* (sleeve of mother of God), *sukienki Matki Boskiej* (dress of Mother of God) and *paluszki Matki Boskiej* (little fingers of the Mother of God). Chopped and scalded with boiling water along with white clover it was given to horses as a protection against many illnesses.

The root of willow gentian was cooked by housewives and the liquid given to cows to help make the butter yellow.

Geranium
Pelargonium
Bodziszek, geranjum, pelargonia

One of the best loved plants in the Polish country cottage, it was often transplanted to a windowsill in the wintertime. In the fine arts, the geranium was a preferred flower motif for Stanisław Wyspiański.

Stanisław Wyspiański was a man of numerous talents steeping every field of life with art. He painted murals, designed stained glass windows, tapestries and furniture, wrote plays, designed interiors, painted and took an interest in printing and typography. He used the geranium in textile designs and in the interior design of the Reception Room at the Cracow Art Club. Red geraniums were painted on the frieze and embroidered on door curtains. Geraniums were the focus of his design in the meeting room of the Cracow Medical Society. The meeting room had a frieze of geraniums. The background for his most famous painting called *Macierzyństwo* (Motherhood) contains geraniums. Stanisław Wyspianski was a keen observer of nature and his studies of flora in the Cracow region are collected in *Herbaria* (his legacy of drawings). One of his most famous works is contained within the Franciscan Church in Cracow. The decoration of this beautiful Gothic church has been acclaimed as among his greatest works. Having studied botany, he painted the interior walls with pansies, lilies, nasturtiums and poppies.

Ginger, Wild
Asarum europaeum
Kopytnik

Found growing wild in the shady forests of Poland, the leaves and root of wild ginger were dried and ground into a rough powder and inhaled as a snuff to treat severe headaches. In small doses, it was used as an expectorant and diuretic. In higher doses, wild ginger was known to cause diarrhea and emesis and the possibility of miscarriage in women. Because of its vomiting properties, country folk used it to try and break someone of their alcohol addiction. Adding it to their drink caused them great nausea and emesis and hopefully discouraged them from drinking.

Gromwell
Lithospermum arvense
Nawrot polny

This plant was found in two archeological digs from the neolithic age in Little Poland and determined to be used both medicinally and cosmetically during that era. In a herbal written in 1845, J. Gerald-Wyżycki wrote "individuals who are pale and wish to artificially color themselves use the root of this plant to give themselves a beautiful color." Subsequently, gromwell was called the "peasant's rouge." Other plants used in cosmetics were *Anchusa officinalis* (no common name) which belongs to the borage family and *Echium rubrum* (viper's bugloss). In the latter plant, the root was dried, ground and then reconsituted by adding a little bit of water and then applied to the cheek. *Onosma echioides*, commonly called golden drop, was another plant whose long root yielded a beautiful red dye when the dried powder was reconsituted with a little oil. The root of *Listera cordata*, called twayblade, was chewed by the women into a mash and then used to blush their cheeks.

Hazel
Corylus avellana
Leszczyna

Hazel is one of the more esteemed trees in Poland and associated with much religious folklore and folktales. The most popular folktale depicts the Holy Family fleeing from King Herod's soldiers after the birth of Jesus. The Blessed Virgin and the infant Jesus hide under its low spreading branches and are saved from King Herod's hired assassins.

Perhaps because of its history of protecting the infant Jesus, the leaves of the hazel were often used in the care of children. They were often added to the bath water. This was done to help the child grow strong and walk early. The leaves were also placed on the head during the bath to protect against boils.

The branches of the hazel were braided into harvest wreaths by the country folks during harvest home celebrations.

Heather
Calluna vulgaris
Wrzos

The month of September in Poland is called *Wrzesień*, taking its name from heather, which blooms profusely in fields and meadows throughout all of Poland at that time of year. It was a plant attractive to bees and honey made from the heather flower was considered something special. An infusion of the dried flowers helped to decrease nervousness, sleeplessness and the pains of rheumatism. It was also recommended as a bath for babies who were failing to thrive.

Hemp
Cannabis sativa
Konopie

"Each bed is girdled with a furrowed border
Where hemp plants stand on guard in serried order,
Like cypresses, all silent, green and tall
Between their leaves no serpent dares to crawl."
—*Pan Tadeusz*

This plant of the Nettle family was widely cultivated in Poland for its oil and fibers. The fibers of hemp were retted, dried and broken on a flax brake—similar to the process used for flax. The thick inner fibers were spun on the spinning wheel and then designated for making sacking or very strong thread. They were often plied together to make rope.

The seeds of this plant yield an oil which both Poles and Russians used extensively in cooking and medications. A nourishing soup was made from the seeds. They were also fed to poultry. The leaves of hemp together with the leaves of calamus were given to the cows if they were off their feed.

The oil obtained from the seeds was felt to be helpful in treating kidney problems.

HEMP SEED OIL

Take 1/2 c. hemp seeds and wash in hot water. Place in mortar, and add sugar and crush into a fine mash. Slowly add a half a glass of boiled and cooled water and the oil emerges. Strain through a cloth. This can be taken a few times a day, and is easy to digest for children and elderly alike.

Henbane
Hyoscyamus niger
Lulek, szaleniec

Henbane is found widely throughout central and southern Europe. All parts of the plant are poisonous. The pale yellow flowers contain dark grey seeds resembling poppy. Old folk healers of Poland boiled these seeds and drank the liquid for sleeplessness. It was also administered for use in toothaches by either chewing the leaves or placing a seed on the tooth. Dried and mixed with tobacco, it was smoked in pipes as a treatment for asthma. Syreniusz recommended the leaves and root of henbane for swelling of the body.

Because of its deadly attributes, it was believed to be a witch's plant.

Hollyhock
Althea rosea
Malva prawoślaz

"And she was ...unweariedly joyful, blossoming all over with gladness, like a rose-bush or an exuberant hollyhock."
—The Peasants: Summer

There is no flower that is more representative of old Polish cottage gardens than the hollyhock. At one time called *babia róża* or, old woman's rose, the single, old-fashioned variety of this plant can be seen growing alongside many an old cottage in Poland, its pink and rose colored flowers accenting the lace curtains in the window. One of its best features is the ability to reseed itself and probably the reason for its popularity in Polish cottage gardens.

The dried flowers were used in old Poland to make a tea that was helpful in ridding one of throat troubles and loosened phlegm in the chest. The dried flowers were generally mixed with some dried mullein flowers. They were also used to bring on menstruation. The root was one of the most popular medications for "stomach colds" and hoarseness.

Hops
Humulus lupulus
Chmiel

"Hop vine, oh hop vine, cluster overhead
Happy the bride for whom your bloom is shed."
—Polish Folk Song

Appearing in folk wedding songs throughout all of Poland, hops is always associated with strong and enduring, as well as with secret, love.

The flowers of the female plant, known as strobiles, were used for medicinal purposes. The dried strobiles were pressed through a fine sieve to obtain a powder useful as a sedative to control painful erections and hysterical episodes in women. Mixed with valerian it was calming and aided sleep.

Hops were also used extensively in beer making in Poland. It was grown predominantly in the Lublin region.

Horseradish
Armoracia rusticana
Chrzan pospolity

Cultivated in Poland since the 12th century, horseradish is one of its oldest condiments as well as its oldest medication. Even during the Jagiellonian Era (1384-1572) horseradish root was offered as the chief condiment in the servant halls. Marcin of Urzędow in his Polish Herbal in 1593 recalls: "Horseradish, a splendid herb in Poland, is practically like pepper."

Syreniusz suggested using it for "headaches—grated and drunk with wine and for chilled stomachs and improving digestion." Others suggest the fresh leaves simply be applied to the forehead for headaches.

In those times, horseradish was used in a syrup with vinegar as a treatment for malaria. At one time, horseradish was taken with beer, wine or tea against scurvy, gout and skin illnesses. Cooked with honey it treated phlegm and hoarseness. Cooked with vinegar and water it was used as a rinse to strengthen the gums. The pulp of the root was used to heal wounds that were filled with pus. Among the peasant populations, the grated root was mixed with flour and fat to make plasters for the aches and pains of rheumatism.

In Polish cottages, the horseradish root was preserved in sand in the root cellar. An ancient Polish condiment for meat was *ćwikła*. This was grated horseradish cooked with red beets that had been grated or cut in slabs.

The fresh juice from the root was also added to milk in the summer to prevent its souring too quickly. Polish country women kept butter fresher longer by wrapping it in horseradish leaves.

Hyssop
Hyssoppus officinalis
Hyzop, józefek

Marcin of Urzędow noted that "hyssop is an excellent herb; scarce is the person who does not have it in his garden." It appeared in Poland in the 16th century and was spread by the Benedictine and Cistercian monks who grew it in the monastery gardens. Older Polish women often pressed fresh branches of hyssop between the pages of their prayer book.

Hyssop was known as a cleansing herb and a tea was made from it to strengthen the lungs and stomach. It was also found to be effective as a gargle for an inflammed throat. The young, new shoots fried in fat were supposed to be an effective treatment for the stomach. For abnormal sweating of the feet, a mix of hyssop, oakbark, horsetail and yarrow was found to be helpful.

In Polish folk medicine, hyssop has been used chiefly to encourage a failing appetite, by drinking a hot tea made from steeping 1 teaspoon of the dried herb in a glass of boiling water.

Hyssop found more favor in the kitchen. Used either fresh or dried, it was added to salads, meat dishes, and bean or potato soup. Strongly aromatic hyssop was grown in the garden to attract bees.

Horsetail
Equisetum arvense
Skrzyp polny

There are nine different varieties of horsetail found in Poland. Syreniusz recommended preparing it with wine for dysentery and bloody lungs. He also suggested it in the form of a bath, compress or as a rub for wounds resulting from duels. It was used in the form of a grated powder mixed with water for ulcers on the liver and uterus and mixed in wine for intestinal wounds and stomach ulcers.

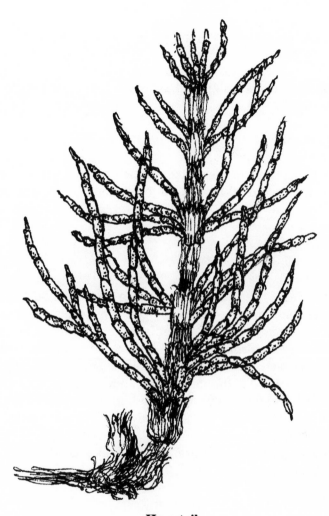

Horsetail

Father Kneipp used it for internal bleeding and bloody emesis. The gypsies of Poland added horsetail to the feed of their horses to strengthen and improve their appetite.

HORSETAIL HERBAL BATH
(for rheumatism, neuralgia and excessive perspiration of feet)

2 qts. water
1 c. horsetail

Boil the horsetail in the water and add to bath water. Bath should not exceed 20 minutes in the evening before bedtime.

Ivy, Ground
Glechoma hederacea
Bluszczyk ziemny, kurdybanek

Better known as a weed among American gardeners, this creeping, trailing plant that spreads extensively through gardens is a native of Europe. More commonly known as gill-over-the-ground, a decoction of the plant decreased phlegm.

The leaves were felt to cleanse the blood and subsequently used in the form of fresh juice in the springtime. They were put through a meat grinder and then squeezed through a cloth to obtain the fresh juice. In the barnyard it was used as a remedy for horses having trouble urinating.

From an old Polish periodical that contained family recipes in the village of Augustow written in 1850 comes this remedy:

BOULLION
(for the chest and cough)

Place in a pot a new chicken, 1/2 of a shoulder blade of veal, a handful each of dried cowslip, coltsfoot and couch grass. Add a gram of ground ivy, a few parsley roots and some barley. Cover the pot with a tight-fitting lid and cook a few hours so that the meat falls apart. Strain through a clean cloth and drink in the morning and evening.

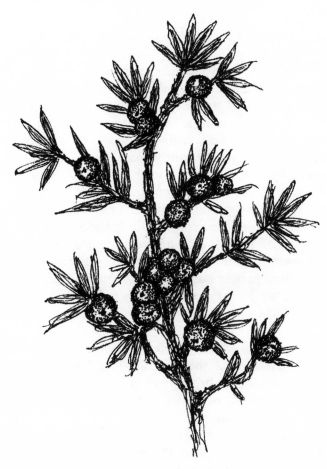

Juniper

Juniper
Juniperus communis
Jałowiec pospolity

"...and upon earthenware tiles there lay juniper berries, smouldering and exhaling their aromatic smoke, filling the cabin with a bluish haze,through which the awful majesty of death was mistily visible. So lay, then, in silent state, the body of Matthias Boryna..."
—*The Peasants: Summer*

POLISH HERBS, FLOWERS & FOLK MEDICINE

This quote from the 1924 Nobel prize winner Reymont's book reflects one of the most common uses of juniper in Polish life—as an incense in church and home. Found in sandy places and pine forests throughout Poland, it was especially prolific in the Kurpie region in Mazowsze. It was a valued wood for making furniture and was the preferred wood for making canes. Lightweight but sturdy enough to lean on, it was used by shepards and travelers not only as a walking device but also as a cudgel and it was even believed to have protective devices against evil powers.

There were many superstitious beliefs centered around juniper. The berries were used as incense to protect the house against evil spirits and "pestilential winds" as well as cattle being sent out to pasture for the first time in the spring. It was, as indicated by the quote, burnt in the room where a dead person was laid-out. A small branch of it placed in a pocket on a long journey would prevent the feet from burning. A branch tucked in a cap or behind a holy picture protected against witchcraft.

The *górale*, the mountain people of southern Poland, made a juice of the juniper berries which they sold to pharmacies to be used against dropsy. A decoction of the berries caused sweating, acted as a diuretic and was used for swelling or kidney stones. A decoction made from the root healed herpes and rashes.

Jam was made from the berries and added to water, milk or wine. Sometimes oil was extracted from the berries as well. Juniper was used extensively in the kitchen when cooking game and making marinades, especially for mushrooms. Smoke from the berries was used for smoking meats. It was often added to cabbage and turnips to decrease their odors while cooking. Parts of butter churns were made of this wood so that the butter would churn better. At one time it was also one of the main ingredients in making beer.

HERBS AND FLOWERS

TO IMPROVE METABOLISM

Ingest 4 juniper berries each day for 15 days adding one each day and then decrease one each day until you are back to four.

TO AWAKEN APPETITE AND IMPROVE DIGESTION

1 Tbsp. juniper berries
1 c. water

Boil the juniper berries in water for 15 minutes. Strain. Drink 1 Tbsp. 2 to 3 times a day after eating.

JUNIPER BEER

Crush 30 lbs. of berries in 10 liters of water with hops added. Continue process for making beer.

Lady's Mantle
Alchemilla vulgaris
Przywrotnik

When hung in a window or thrown into the fire, a wreath made from this herb would disperse storm clouds.

Larkspur
Delphinium elatum
Ostróżka

A mainstay of Polish cottage gardens, this flower was both attractive to look at and favored by bees. The Polish housewife also placed leaves of larkspur beneath her bedsheets to deter fleas. The root of larkspur was drunk with milk for weak hearts.

Lavender
Lavandula augustifolia
Lawenda

Lavender became very popular in Europe during the Middle Ages when it was used to treat a variety of ailments including arthritis, gout and broken limbs. Marcin of Urzędow stated: "Everyone knows of lavender because all the ladies grow it in their garden." His other comments ascertained that "the oil of lavender is good to rub beneath the nose." Syreniusz recalled that it "removes chills from dampness, nausea and headache when a woman wears it beneath her cap." For headaches, a wine was mixed·with lavender on its own or in a mixture with sage, rosemary, marjoram, thyme and lavender, noting: "It warms a cold brain and weak stomach and decreases dizziness." Lavender wine was supposed to strengthen the heart and protect against nausea.

During the Middle Ages, a very popular item in Poland was called *lavendogra*, made from lavender and rosemary. *Lavendogra* was the Polish translation of L'eau de la reine d'Hongrie, or Queen of Hungary water. In its time, *lavendogra* was lauded by Elizabeth, the sister of Kazimierz the Great (1333-1370) who at age 72 cured herself of gout and rheumatism using Hungary water. Acting as regent for her son (King Louis of Hungary) in Poland, she generated a great deal of amazement by washing not only her face but her entire body in it and supposedly becoming younger looking every day.

Lavender was useful in awakening a poor appetite, for rheumatism, and as an antiseptic. The oil, massaged into the skin, was said to rid one of lice.

LAVENDOGRA

1/2 c. lavender
1 c. rosemary leaves
95% proof alcohol

Cover lavender dried rosemary leaves with alcohol. Place in

a dark area for two weeks. Strain, dilute with equal amounts of boiled and cooled water. Pour into dark bottles and cork, storing away from light. Instead of dried leaves, the fresh can be used; just remember to use twice the amount of rosemary to lavender. Sometimes 1/2 c. mint is added.

Lemon Balm
Melissa officinalis
Melisa lekarska, rojownik

Lemon balm's other Polish names of *miodownik*, honey plant, and *pszczelnik*, bee plant, indicate its use to attract bees to the garden. The inside of the beehive was rubbed with lemon balm before it was put out for bees. Marcin of Urzędow recalls that "the bees find it a real delight...it is good to have this herb near bees." The country housewife carried it in her apron pocket when going to market to sell her butter and eggs believing that it would bring buyers "swarming around her, like bees in a hive."

Syreniusz recommended lemon balm for headaches, heart and stomach ailments, mushroom poisoning as well as for rheumatism and asthma. Its other attributes included: "It gladdens the heart, works well for those sad and melancholy and warms the stomach." Taken at night, lemon balm was said to "remove from the body melancholy blood, nightmares and make one merry."

It was used for a variety of purposes including cramps, asthma, anemia, to regulate menstruation and improve digestion and appetite. For those who had a break in the skin as a result of a rusty nail, the flower was soaked in spirytus and applied to the puncture. The crushed leaves of lemon balm were prepared as a compress for the pains of gout and trauma. In some villages, an infusion of lemon balm and marjoram was drunk to strengthen memory. The leaves, gathered and dried before the plant flowered, were used as a teas for migraines and to strengthen the nerves.

Lemon Balm

LEMON BALM BATH
(for rheumatism pain)

2-3 tsp. lemon balm
1 quart water

Boil together for 2 minutes. Strain. Add to bath water.

LEMON BALM BATH

1/4 c. dried lemon balm
1/4 c. dried yarrow
1/4 c. wormwood
1/4 c. peppermint
1/4 c. marjoram
1/4 c. pine needles
1/4 c. sweet flag root

Make a mixture of the above ingredients. Boil together in 10 quarts of water for 30 minutes under a tight lid. The bath should not be prolonged over 20 minutes at 37-38 degrees C.

LEMON BALM DRINK
(for relief of mental stress, problems sleeping in the elderly, increasing appetite and improving digestion)

1 tsp. dried lemon balm
1 c. boiling water

Steep lemon balm in boiling water. Drink half a glass 2 to 3 times a day.

Lily of the Valley
Convallaria majalis
Konvalia

Possessing incredible fragrance, this low-growing plant makes dense carpets in Polish forests. Although it is not a plant used currently for home medication because of its poisonous properties, it was nonetheless used in old Poland. Sixteenth century herbals mention a wine made from the flowers used for epilepsy. Among county folk, the flowers were boiled for a tea and given to children in weakened form as a remedy for worms. The root of this plant was also used as a wash for the skin. The

131

root was dug and ground into a fine powder. An infusion was made from the powder into a wash for the skin by women who wished to add smoothness and luster to their face. The root of *Polygonatum officinale*, commonly called Solomon's seal, was also used in the same manner.

Lily, Madonna
Lilium candidum
Lilja

Associated with Blessed Virgin Mary and purity, the madonna lily was grown in Polish monastic gardens for centuries and used both for decorating the church and as a healing herb. It was a flower that brought forth numerous images. Beautiful girls were likened to it: "She stood, like a white lily near the road," as were unhappy orphans: "Tearful, like a white lily, which a wind flutters." The white flower petals were placed on areas of the body that were burnt. The root of the lily, grated, mixed with honey and applied to a wart will make it go away.

Lily, Turk's Cap
Lilium martagon
Złotogłów

The most naturally abundant of all lilies, *lilium martagon* is native to much of Europe, ranging from southern Europe to Siberia and Mongolia. It is naturalized in the Tatra highlands of Poland and is one of the chief flower motifs used by the mountain people in their arts and crafts especially the folk dress of the mountain women. The color of the flower is a soft pinkish-purple with darker spots. It is currently under the protected plant species of Poland.

Linden
Tilia cordata
Lipa drobnolista

Linden is one of the most frequently planted trees in Polish gardens. From ancient times, linden was considered a sacred tree. It protected against lightning and evil spirits. It was a place to leave offerings to the gods and conduct ritual dances. Later, after the advent of Christianity, the tree was dedicated to the Blessed Virgin Mary and many roadside shrines were hung on its trunk. In early Poland many kings held war councils and judgements beneath this tree. King Jan Sobieski became enamored of it and had it planted at Wilanów. In later times, Jan Kochanowski (1530-1584) known as the father of Polish poetry, wrote his verses beneath a linden tree. One of his poems is written for and about the linden tree. In the first stanza, the linden speaks to a guest resting beneath its shady leaves saying, "And I, with my quiet rustling, can easily induce a sweet dream." In the next stanza, the linden asks the poet for an ode. In the third stanza, the linden tells the poet it is withering away from being "courted with bad poetry."

Linden was a tree of inestimable value. It was used in woodcarvings especially shrines and holy figures and in the making of musical instruments. From its inner bark, rough shoes called *chodaki* were made as well as baskets and hats. The magnificent altar of St. Mary's in Cracow is made from linden. From its seeds, an oil was extracted for consumptives and for use in oil lamps. It made for wonderful honey. And if that wasn't enough, the people of the Kujawy region say that a devil can be tied up with the inner bark of the linden.

All the parts of the tree were useful in Polish folk medicine. The bark and leaves were applied to the eyes and to inflamed areas of skin. For headaches, the leaves were applied to the head and a tea made from the flowers. It was also supposed to be helpful for hair loss and was known as a general panacea for nerve troubles. In old apothecaries, a distillation of the flower was supposedly effective for convulsions and epilepsy.

In traditions among the nobility, a linden was planted on the day of the birth of a child.

LINDEN DRINK
(for calming nerves and inducing sleep)

1 Tbps. linden flowers
1 qt. water

Boil the linden flowers in water for 15 minutes. Steep and drink one-half glass 3 to 4 times a day. Honey or raspberry syrup can be added for flavoring.

LINDEN BATH
(to sooth and induce sleep)

2 to 3 c. dried linden flowers
1 qt. water

Boil together the linden flowers and water for 20 minutes. Strain and add to bath water.

LINDEN BLOSSOM COOLER

6 Tbsp. dried linden flowers
5 c. water
6 Tbsp. honey (optional)

Add dried linden blossoms to boiling water. Set aside covered. When the dried herbs drop to the bottom, strain. Add honey to taste. Chill and serve.

HERBS AND FLOWERS

Lovage
Levisticum officinale
Lubczyk ogrodowy

It is known that Kazimierz the Great (1333-1370) grew lovage in his garden. In this period, lovage was used as a treatment against dog bites, snake and scorpion bites. It was also felt to be an aphrodisiac. Slavic girls wove it in their wedding wreathes or hid it in the folds of their wedding dresses or hair, believing that it would guarantee happiness throughout their married life. It was supposed to grant protection against witchcraft and bad weather, thought to be most effective during a full moon.

Medicinally lovage improved digestion, promoted menstruation and eased the pangs of childbirth. A very common drink for this purpose was a cordial made from alcohol and fresh seeds.

In the kitchen, the fresh and dried leaves were added to soups, sauces, meats and salads. The fresh leaves have a more intensive flavor. It can still be seen today growing in many modern Polish gardens.

Marjoram
Origanum majorana
Majeranek, majeran ogrodowy

Marjoram was brought to Poland in the 16th century during the time of the Renaissance and became extremely popular both in the kitchen and stillroom. Syreniusz recalls that it was "sown and planted on windows in various pots."

Prepared in wine, marjoram was used for headaches. Powdered marjoram mixed with honey was applied to bruises and breaks. It could induce menstruation and was felt to be soothing for inflammed eyes. Marjoram crushed in the fingers and brought to the nose could decrease sneezing, drive away colds, clear the head, sharpen intellect and return memory. It was especially helpful in assisting digestion and listless livers and pancreas. In old Poland, marjoram was used as an herb in fatty meats such as goose, pork-joints, meat pies and stuffings. It helped

135

improve the taste of bean and tripe soups and ease their digestion. It was a main ingredient in sausage making and often used as a substitute for salt.

Marigold
Calendula officinalis
Nagietek lekarski

Marigold could be found growing in Polish gardens from ancient times. Its sunny color was much loved in the garden. In the 16th century Syrenuisz wrote that, "All the country folk know marigold. The flower follows the turn of the sun...perhaps that is why it is called the 'country clock.' Marcin of Urzędow wrote: "Everyone knows that marigold is called wreath, which they use to weave wreaths."

Besides noting its usefulness as a timepiece, Syreniusz recommended it as an effective remedy for "difficulty breathing and excessive bile." It was used to scare away the evil eye, protect against ill winds and contagious fevers. Its juices were used to bring on menses. The fresh leaves were applied to all warts. It was also an important remedy for external wounds. The flower fried in butter with comfrey made a salve for healing wounds and reducing swollen glands. A tea was made from the dry petals which was good for the digestive system and strengthened the heart.

In olden times the petals were used to color butter and cheese by adding the crushed petals to milk or cream. Cheaper than the costly saffron, it was also added to baked breads and cakes to create a beautiful golden color. It also dyed fabrics, textiles, and hair—if mixed with small amounts of lye. The petals could forecast the weather: if the petals of marigold are arranged parallel to the ground before 9 a.m. it means that the day will be nice.

HERBS AND FLOWERS

MARIGOLD INFUSION
(for wounds, bruises and x-ray burns)

1 Tbsp marigold petals
1 c. boiling water

Cover petals with boiling water and allow to steep for 10 minutes. This can be used internally by ingesting one half-glass twice a day. For compresses for these conditions take 4 Tbsp. of petals, cover with one cup cold water and boil gently for 20 minutes in a covered pot.

Marshmallow
Althaea officinalis
Ślaz lekarski

A decoction of the root was drunk as a tea for a cough, cold or difficulty breathing. Fresh leaves were applied to sores and boils. For swollen glands at the neck, the leaves of marshmallow are steeped and applied to the neck. A light decoction of marshmallow and chamomile is used to wash wounds on horses, cows and pigs. Marshmallow, chopped fine with mint and anise, then mixed with fat and rye flour, was spread on a paper and cloth and applied to a hernia.

The flowers of marshmallow and linden steeped with honey produced an excellent cure for colds.

Melilot
Melilotus albus
Nostrzyk biały

The folk name for this plant *urokowe ziele* or "spell plant" indicates its use in magical beliefs and practices at one time. The villagers used it to incense either a person or animal who had been given the evil eye.

An infusion was used to make an eye-wash and was also prepared in spring with wine, called May wine.

Mistletoe
Viscum album
Jemioła biała

In his herbal, Father Kneipp noted that mistletoe grew in the woods of the castles at Tęczyn, near Cracow, where it could be gathered. It was also plentiful in the woods in the Poznań region where it was felt to be one of the best protections against witches. In order to calm a cow that tended to kick, they made her a crown of mistletoe three times. On the Feast of St. Mark, they placed mistletoe in the pig's trough to protect it against illness.

Monkshood
Aconitum napellus
Tojad

This flower and herb can be found growing wild in the Tatra mountains as well as carefully cultivated in cottage gardens in that region. This sun-loving plant is called Slippers of the Blessed Mother in Poland. It contains poisonous alkaloids that increase the action of the heart.

Mountain Ash
Sorbus aucuparia
Jarząb pospolity, jarzębina

Sometimes called *skorus* by the mountain people of southern Poland, there are at least five different varieties of this tree in Poland. In some localities, it is forbidden to eat the berries of mountain ash and considered a sin to cut down a mountain ash because of beliefs that, at one time, it was a woman who was turned into a tree by a mean mother-in-law. Another folk belief said that a branch of mountain ash hung over the bed of a young man or woman harboring "immodest desires" would squelch them.

The flower was used as a diuretic and to loosen bowels, especially in children. The berries were used for bloody stools and illnesses of the lungs, liver and kidney.

Mugwort
Artemisia vulgaris
Bylica

This plant had an infinite variety of uses in and around the house. Mugwort collected from nine different fields would increase a woman's fertility. In the Kielce area, a baby was bathed in mugwort and thyme in order to give the child strength. In the Radom area, mugwort was tucked in the eaves of the house in order to protect it against "uncleanliness" on St. John's Eve. Both mugwort and wormwood were placed in the coffin in the belief that it would delay decomposition of the body. Mugwort could also ward off the evil eye, making it a good idea to carry a sprig of it at all times on St. John's Eve.

If a person experienced a terrible fright, they could develop epilepsy. The variety of treatments for this disorder included incensing the individual by burning flax and hemp and drenching the person suddenly with cold water. Immediately thereafter they were given a decoction of mugwort.

Young maidens often made a belt of mugwort to wear around their waist while singing and dancing around the midsummer fire. They believed that this would ease pains in the lower back.

A persistent problem that plagued many a household in Poland was the intrusion of flies. A few long branches of mugwort were sprinkled with sour milk and hung from a beam generally near the ceiling of the house. The flies then clustered on the branch and stopped plaguing the inhabitants. When enough flies had settled on the branch, two people cautiously approached it with an open sack and captured the insects. The sack would then be taken outside and disposed of.

The country villagers wiped their hands in mugwort in order to keep the bees from stinging.

Mullein
Verbascum thapsus
Dziewanna

Mullein's ability to grow in sandy, unfertile places where little of value tends to grow gave rise to a Polish folk song which states: "Where mullein grows in abundance, the maidens are poor."

In one of the first Polish herbals of the 16th century Marcin Siennik wrote: "Spirytus with the flowers of this plant protects against spells and dispels evil spirits." It was often used in weather predictions: if the flowers were large and covered the entire stalk, the winter would be strong with much snow and vice versa.

Syreniusz believed that numerous parts of the plant were useful. The root in the form of a powder added to liquor was good for the lungs and for diarrhea. For a "four-day fever" the juice from the root was drunk, mixed with malmsey wine. For toothache, "the warm root held by the lips" and chopped and cooked in vinegar was a mouthwash. For warts, the juice from the leaves and flowers were rubbed on warts and an infusion from them was used for burning eyes. For burns, apply the fresh leaf; sore feet were bathed in an infusion made from the flower and plantain leaves.

In treating dysentery and diarrhea, an infusion of the flower was used as an enema. An infusion made from both the flower and the dried root served as a diuretic for kidney stones and gout. Used in a bath, such an infusion was a help for hemorroids. A powder made from the dried flowers was used as a dusting for cracked nipples in breastfeeding mothers after first being moistened with carrot juice. Syreniusz also believed that the oil obtained from the flowers of mullein "works miracles for the hair" and that a decoction from the flowers colors it golden.

A decoction from the flowers of mullein mixed with alum yields a yellow/green color. For dyeing yarn, the wool is soaked in water and vinegar for 48 hours, to which the liquid from the flowers is added.

Mustard, Black
Brassica nigra
Gorczyca czarna

Black mustard is native to Europe and has been cultivated as a condiment and healing plant for thousands of years. The day-to-day expense accounts of King Jagiello listed black mustard as being grown on the King's estates. The seeds were ground up in mortars, mixed with water and vinegar and made into a mustard for use with various meats.

The ground up seeds were also used to make plasters and poultices for the chest and any body part that could benefit from the application of heat.

Myrtle
Myrtus communis
Mirt

Myrtle is a small shrubby plant that should not be confused with periwinkle, the trailing ground cover. It was generally grown indoors in pots on windowsills along with scented rose geraniums by young unmarried women. The bride's head piece on her wedding day was often made of myrtle. Many photographs of old Polish weddings reveal a bride with sprigs of myrtle on her hemline. It often also served as a boutonniere for the groom to wear in his lapel. Any girl who grew her own plant would never give it away or she would lose her luck.

Nasturtium
Tropaeolum majus
Nasturcja

This herb and flower has come to be associated with one of Poland's best loved poets. Born of peasant stock, Jan Kasprowicz (1860-1926) was familiar with hunger, poverty and social injustice. In his later years he bought a home in Zakopane in the south of Poland and planted nasturtium in the flowerboxes on the porch and at the windows. They became the subject matter of the last verse of his last book and the title of one of his biographies. There, in the tranquility of the mountains, he wrote until he died. Upon his death, his wife completely surrounded his body with the flowers he so loved. To this day, his mountain home, called Harenda, has been preserved just as it was during his lifetime, complete with nasturtiums in all the window boxes.

Nettle
Urtica dioica
Pokrzywa zwyczajna

Nettle can be found growing all over Poland. Slavic people have attributed magical properties to it since ancient times. On the day of Midsummer's Eve, it was hung above the entrance to the house to protect against demons. If a storm was approaching, they would burn nettle, thinking it would disperse the clouds and protect against lightning. In the 12th century it was used in textile manufacturing and clothes made from its fibers were worn to frighten away demons. Nettle thread was used in Poland from ancient times up until the 17th century when it was replaced by silk.

Syreniusz felt it was a herb that was helpful in many situations. The leaves steeped in wine "cleansed the stomach, removed rumblings of the intestines and young nettle cooked with snails softened the stomach." The seeds of nettle drunk with wine cured mushroom and hemlock poisoning and poisonous bites.

For gout, a salve was made from bear fat along with the crushed leaves and seeds of nettle. The crushed leaves placed into the nose would stop bleeding. An old Polish calendar suggested: to keep from exhaustion while dancing or walking long distances, place in your shoes, under the sole, the leaf of nettle.

The fresh leaves were drunk as a healthful tonic or to fortify one against colds and flu. It was also used as a diuretic, blood cleanser and healer of liver ailments, gallbladder troubles, irregular menstruation, diarrhea and even nerve conditions. Steeping the leaves and root in spirytus was beneficial in treating hair loss, graying hair as well as dandruff. It was rubbed into the hair at night.

NETTLE LINAMENT
(for rhuematism)

2 tsp. nettle root
1/2 qt. vodka

Allow the root to steep in one half quart of vodka and allow to stand for 6 to 8 days. Rub on aching areas.

Farmyard animals could also benefit from nettle. If given to chickens, it would increase their weight, harden their eggshells, deepen the color of the yolk and increase egg laying.

NATURAL FERTILIZER

8 to 10 lbs. nettle
50 qts. water

Mix nettle with water amd allow to ferment for 14 days. When finished use in 1:10 proportions, i.e., 1 cup to 10 cups water and use in garden.

Oak
Quercus robur
Dąb

Not too far from Cracow, in a town called Kazimierz on the Wisła River, there are oak trees that are one thousand years old. Revered since ancient times, the oak has always been a symbol of strength. It was recommended that the weak and debilitated, suffering from consumption and rheumatism, bathe in an infusion made from the bark of oak. Water in which the bark had soaked was used in washing wounds. It was also used to rinse the mouth when teeth were hurting.

The wood from the oak, known to be durable and long lasting, was used for making posts on which to hang roadside shrines and crucifixes. The oak bark was used to obtain a black or brown dye for coloring eggs called *pisanki* during Easter time. Bread was baked on oak leaves to keep the bottoms from burning. Acorns were cooked and used to make a coffee during hard times and also as a treatment for dysentery.

Oats
Avena sativa
Owies

"Withal, her head began to ache, and she had to put a warm oatmeal poultice sprinkled with vinegar on the top of her head, before it passed off."
—*The Peasants: Autumn*

A traditional food staple of Poland for both man and beast, the whole plant was gathered when the grains were ripe. The grain was separated from the lower portion, the straw, and used as food staple. The lower portion, the oat straw was cooked and cooled enough to soak tired and aching feet. It was also used to treat eczema and headaches.

Onion
Allium cepa
Cebula

Besides being a culinary staple, the onion was used to treat ulcerous and hard-to-heal wounds, boils and sores. There were a variety of methods used. One was to cut the onion in slices and apply it directly to the wound. Another was to chop it very fine, run through a food mill, and apply the resulting mash to the wound.

For children who were wan, listless and had poor appetite, an onion syrup was recommended. Onions were chopped very fine and covered with sugar or honey. The mixture was allowed to stand in a warm place for a few days. It was then squeezed through a cheesecloth. One tablespoon of the resulting juice was taken straight or added to tea three to five times a day. Polish herbalist Falimirz suggested onion syrup for hair growth by massaging the head with it. He also recommended that "syrup from the onion dropped in the ear reduces sharp screeching noises in the ear.

Oregano/Wild marjoram
Origanum vulgare
Lebiodka, dziki majeranek

During the Middle Ages in Poland, oregano was believed to protect against illness and withcraft, used to treat poisonous bites, decrease sex drive, erotomania and hysteria. This herb was also used to treat headaches, excessive sweating and to strengthen the appetite. Added to bath water, it helped ease the pains of rheumatism. It was also considered one of the most important herbs for treating animal illnesses and often given to cows after birthing.

Growing wild all across Poland, it has been used in dyeing wools and textiles; the flower as well as the leaves give a red, orange or brown color. It was one of the most important herbs to be blessed on August 15.

Oregano Drink
(for difficulty digesting and chronic burping)

1 cup wild marjoram (oregano)
1/2 cup peppermint
1/4 cup root of goats beard

Add 1 tsp. of mixture to a glass of boiling water and drink 1/2 glass after eating.

Pansy
Viola tricolor
Bratek

There were at one time fifteen different varieties of pansy growing wild throughout all of Poland. For scrofula, children drank a tea made from the dried flowers of pansy or bathed in it in order to get well. An infusion of the dried flowers mixed with chamomile and raspberry leaves made a hearty tea for colds and influenza.

Parsley
Petroselinum sativum
Pietruszka

The leaves and root of parsley were already being used in Poland in the 16th century and grown both in the garden and in pots on windowsills. For treatment of hernias, a plaster was made from parsley, southernwood and fat and applied to the groin. If one suffered from a swollen abdomen, an application of the fresh leaves of parsley and a drink made from the leaves reduced the swelling.

Fresh parsley leaves were a constant standby in the Polish kitchen. A couple of stalks thrown into a pot of boiling potatoes, enhanced their flavor especially if they were a bit old and wrinkled. Chopped finely, they were sprinkled on a batch of new potatoes. It was added to soups and vegetables and meats of all kinds. Dried carefully and stored in cloth bags, it added flavor to the monotonous winter fare.

Peppermint
Mentha piperita
Mięta pieprzowa

"..its inhabitants looked out upon the world again, gratefully inhaling the cool air and the scents of the land after the rain, especially those of the young birches and the mint-plants in the gardens."
—*The Peasants: Spring*

There are many varieties of mint in Poland but the one that consistantly seems to surface in Polish folk medicine is peppermint. As throughout the rest of the world, mints have always played a critical role in aiding and abetting digestion. Cooked in milk, it was drunk hot for stomach cramps. Syreniusz states "Drunk in red wine, it will stop hiccups, vomiting and coughing fits and also warm the stomach." He also suggested treating bites from bees and hornets with the juice of mint or an application of the crushed leaves. Fresh leaves applied to the forehead were helpful for treating headaches and hangovers. For pus filled wounds, a special plaster was made from potato flour and either the dried herb or its juice. A strong peppermint tea was used to rinse and freshen the mouth. Chewing on a peppermint leaf was a simpler method of freshing the breath.

Of all its uses, it was proclaimed the best herb for pain and cramps of the stomach. For hernias a mixture of peppermint, anise and marshmallow were chopped fine and mixed with rye flour to make a salve. Spread on paper or cloth it was applied to hurt areas.

Father Kneipp recommended it for the coughing-up of blood. He suggested mixing peppermint with horsetail in equal proportions to make a tea. Add a drop of lemon and drink 1 tsp. every hour.

147

Periwinkle
Vinca Minor
Barwinek

Periwinkle is an herb that has numerous associations. It played an important role in the traditional making of wreaths throughout the seasonal year, especially that of Corpus Christi. It was also closely associated with death customs and planted on graves in the cemetery.

When it came to healing purposes, a decoction of the leaves was added to bath water as a treatment for rheumatism and for washing wounds. Taken internally as a tea, periwinkle helped prevent scurvy. Soaked in wine, it reduced headaches.

Plantain
Plantago lanceolata
Babka lancetowata

From the most distant of times, old country women knew that the healing properties of plantain were in the fresh leaves. It was best known for its efficacy in treating skin disorders in both humans and animals. The fresh, crushed leaves were applied to cuts, burns, furuncles and inflammations of the skin, then wrapped in a clean cloth. This procedure was repeated daily until healing. Another method was to mix the crushed leaves with lard, salt and soft bread and then apply to ulcers and boils. The juice of the leaves was used against fevers and bee stings. The crushed leaves mixed with egg white were applied to snake bites. The leaves of plantain was also used to treat whooping cough, bronchial asthma, tuberculosis, internal bleeding, and as an anti-inflammatory in fevers and rheumatism. While fresh was considered best, the leaves were also effective when gathered and dried during flowering.

Plantain

In Romania, plantain was used in spring salads during the Lenten season. The Lithuanians made a wine with the juice of leaves as a medication for internal bleeding. In Polish folk medicine, plantain was known as an effective remedy for ills of mucous membranes and for cleansing of the blood. A fresh, tapered root of plantain was placed in the ear for toothaches and removed only when blackened.

Poppy, Opium
Papaver somniferum
Mak ogrodowy

"Cradled in leaves, in grasses swaddled deep,
As when a noisy child is laid to sleep,
His mother ties green curtains o'er his head
And sprinkles poppy leaves beneath his head."
—*Pan Tadeusz*

Putting poppy leaves under the head of an infant was typical in many parts of Poland including Galicia, the partitioned section of Poland under Austria-Hungary. A variety of sources also indicate that the top of the poppy plant was boiled and a spoonful of the liquid given to crying babies who had difficulty falling asleep.

Poppy, Field
Papaver rhoeas
Mak polny

The corn poppy was originally a native of Asia but now grows wild in Europe and in Poland. The seeds from this plant were used extensively in the baking of cakes, pastries, breads and rolls. The seeds were also ground into an oil and used extensively during the Lenten season. A decoction was drunk as a treatment for whooping cough. Among the country women, who could ill afford the cost of cosmetics, a poppy petal rubbed against the cheek acted as a rouge.

Primrose, Evening
Oenothera biennis
Wiesołek dwuletni

This sweet smelling flower opens in the evening and closes in the morning. It was used for treating eczema of the face. The flower was soaked in water and the water then applied to the face. Frying the flower in butter and applying it to the face as a salve, once it had cooled, was another trusted method in Polish folk medicine.

Raspberry
Rubus idaeus
Malina właściwa

In the early Middle Ages, raspberry bushes could be seen growing in the monastery gardens in southern Europe and Poland. In the 16th century, the monks began making a raspberry syrup that was used as restorative.

Syreniusz recommended the raspberry flower mixed with honey and water "to wash eyes that are swollen and draining" and to mix the juice of the leaves with honey as a treatment for asthma. The leaves cooked in wine and drunk with honey was to heal "ulcerous lungs." Prepared as a tea, raspberry was a medicine for jaundice and kidney stones. The dried leaves were utilized for compresses and poultices while the fresh leaves were made into salves.

There is no scene more characteristic during a summer in Poland than the marketplace piled with heap upon heap of red raspberries. Eagerly bought up by housewives, they were made into syrups, compotes, wine, preserves and liqueurs. It was used in making pierogies, soups and as a filling between layers of cakes. The dried leaves and stems were often added to teas of poor quality to improve the taste.

RASPBERRY DRINK
(for prolonged diarrhea)

1 tsp. dried raspberry leaves
1 1/2 c. water

Cover leaves with water and boil. Strain and drink one half glass 3 times a day.

Rhubarb
Rheum
Rumbarbarum

Found growing in practically all cottage gardens, rhubarb was cooked with water and sugar and then cooled to make a thirst quenching drink. It was also mixed with other seasonal fruits to make a compote as a dessert. Medicinally, the raw leaves of rhubarb were applied to the head to cure headaches.

Rose
Rosa gallica, rosa centifolia
Róża

Grown in Polish medieval gardens, roses were often likened to young beautiful girls: "There emerged a young girl, like a flowering rose."

From a pharmacopeia called *Pharmacopea Cracoviensis* (Cracow Pharmacopeia) written in 1683 by Jan Woyno, court physician of Jan Sobieski, we find the names of these two roses which were grown in the gardens of Cracow and used for medicinal purposes. The fresh leaves, crushed to a pulp in a mortar and mixed with sugar was an excellent remedy for consumptive lungs, especially if taken with a tea made from barley water. The juice extracted from the flower petals, boiled in wine and soaked on a rag, cooled burning eyes.

Both of these roses are known as old European roses, i.e. garden varieties that were grown in Europe before the coming of the China roses at the end of the 18th century. The *gallica* roses date back numerous centuries as descendents of the wild *Rosa gallica* that is native to southern and central Europe. A common name for it is the French rose. *Rosa gallica* is a small shrub and popular in Polish cottage gardens where space was at a premium. Its variety, the "Apothecary's Rose" (*Rosa gallica* var. *officinalis*), with fragrant, scarlet flowers is one of the oldest forms (dating back to the 1600's) of *Rosa gallica* in cultivation.

    Rosa centifolia was one of the first roses to be cultivated and domesticated. It is generally called the cabbage rose, the name originating from the bottom petals flexing out like the lower leaves of a cabbage. It, too, is a hardy, compact bush whose flowers have an arresting fragrance. Even though these roses have been surpassed in popularity by the hybrid teas, both antique roses present such an ancient tradition in Polish gardening that they should be restored to garden use.

Rose, Wild
Rosa canina
Róża dzika

Like the ancient Romans, Marcin Siennik, in his herbal, suggests using the flowers of the wild rose to make a pillow that is soothing and induces sleep. Syreniusz suggested using rose hips for bloody coughs, bloody emesis and diarrhea. It was also used to halt excessive menstrual bleeding.

    Father Kneipp suggested making a marmalade of the fruit and/or using the rose hips to make a tea for cleansing the kidney and bladder. The country folk clearly used it according to the doctrine of signatures. For any redness or flushing of the face, the flower was soaked in water and applied with a cloth. Sometimes the flowers were fried in butter and also applied to the face.

ROSE PETAL SYRUP

1 c. rose petals
4 c. boiling water
5 c. sugar

Cover rose petals with boiling water and let sit for 24 hours. After filtering add sugar and boil. Collect off the foam until it thickens. Place in a cool spot and add a teaspoon to tea twice a day.

Rosemary
Rosmarinus officinalis
Rozmaryn lekarski

When you win my love
You will have my hand
And a garland of rosemary
From my garden fair.

I shall offer it
To you my dear love
I shall place it on the altar
At the wedding mass. —*Polish folk song*

In many regions of Poland rosemary was a plant associated with engagements and weddings. This was especially true in the Poznan region. Newly engaged men would wear a branch of rosemary tucked behind a green ribbon wound around their hats on the left side. On the day of the wedding the groomsmen would wear rosemary in their hats and the groom had a boutonniere made of rosemary with a white ribbon on the left side of his chest. The bride and bridesmaids also wore

Rosemary

wreaths of rosemary on their head. Similar to rue, it was one time used during the wedding ceremony. Wreaths of rosemary were exchanged between the bride and groom instead of rings.

In old Poland it was also valued as a medicinal plant. Often grown on windowsills, oil of rosemary was used in many cosmetics and added to soaps and shampoo. Wine was made from the flower as well as syrups and confections.

Rue
Ruta graveolens
Ruta

"Near him a girl in green like lowly rue
Looks up to him with eyes as violets blue."
—*Pan Tadeusz*

From the most ancient of times in Poland, rue has been associated with virtuous young maidens. It was an herb cultivated by both young country girls as well as those of the gentry and nobility as a symbol of maidenhood and their availability for marriage. The young girls planted rue in the garden so any passer-by, seeing the herb growing in the garden, would know that within the house there lived a girl of marriageable age.

The rue that the young girl grew in her garden would later play an important role in her engagement and wedding ceremonies. In medieval Poland, wreaths of rue were exchanged between the engaged couple as a symbol of their willingness to enter into the marriage contract. Later on, the exchange of wreaths entered the actual marriage ceremony, where, instead of rings, the priest blessed and exchanged wreaths of rue between the young couple.

Rue was also used to decorate the wedding cake, the hats of the groom and groomsmen and the whip used on the horses that pulled the wagon carrying the bride to church for the wedding. As a talisman for young girls, rue had no equal. When a young unmarried girl died, a wreath of rue was often added to her coffin.

Medicinally, rue was useful in a variety of ways. Father Kneipp recommended that the leaves and flowers be made into a tea to increase appetitie and digestion. This tea was helpful with such problems as difficulty in catching one's breath, a strongly beating heart, cramping, weakness and hysteria. His herbal recommended using rue in very small quantities.

Sage
Salvia officinalis
Szałwia lekarska

Of the 500 types of sage found in the world, only two—*salvia officinalis* and *salvia sclarea*—are used in Polish folk medicine. In France, during the Middle Ages, sage was considered a holy plant tied to the cult of the Blessed Virgin Mary. It was brought to Poland from France in the 16th century by the Cistercian and Benedictine orders. Three sage leaves ingested in the morning were thought to protect one the whole day "against the plague and pestilential airs." During these times it was also prepared with wine or sometimes water to which vinegar had been added. It was an effective remedy for an unrelenting hiccough. In the Poznan area, sage was used for sore throats by making an infusion, adding a little honey and vinegar and gargling with it.

The dried herb was crumbled into the food of someone suffering from stomach troubles. He/she was also offered sage tea. In cooking it was added to food to provide flavor for many tasteless dishes.

St. John's Wort

St. John's Wort
Hypericum perforatum
Dziurawiec zwyczajny, dzwonki Panny Marii (Bells of Blessed Mother),
ziele Św. Jana (herb of St. John), *krewka Matki Boskiej* (blood of
Blessed Mother)

HERBS AND FLOWERS

Commonly found throughout all of Poland in valleys and mountainsides, St. John's wort was one of the twenty different herbs discovered in the archeological digs at Biskupin.

A tall plant, it has yellow flowers which yield a reddish juice resembling blood when squeezed. During the Middle Ages and later, there were many beliefs and superstitions about St. John's wort, including that it cured 99 illnesses and was helpful against magic and evil forces. When it blossomed on St. John's Eve (June 24) a wreath was woven from the plant and flower and various predictions were made according to the intensity of the juice and its color. Hung in the window, it protected the house against lightning. Up until the beginning of the 20th century, it also was believed to protect a new mother and infant against evil spirits when tucked into crevices and the chimney. For this same reason, the midwife often tucked a sprig of this plant under the new mother's pillow and hung some around the neck of the infant until the child's first bath. This was especially true in and around the rural countryside of Cracow.

By the 16th century, it was used as a diuretic and for healing wounds, burns and ulcers. The fresh flowers were soaked in spirytus and applied to new wounds as well as old ones refusing to heal. Following the Doctrine of Signatures, its red color was used to heal internal bleeding. This same red color from the flowers made it useful in dyeing fabrics.

Savory, Summer
Satureja hortensis
Cząber, comber, modrak

Marcin of Urzędow wrote that "savory is a common herb and much eaten in Poland." According to folklore, it provided magical strength and awakened the desire to perform deeds of bravery and valor. It also fell into the category of aphrodisiacs.

In medicinal use, it helped in the digestion of food by awakening secretion of gastric juices as well as stimulating and increasing appetite. In cooking, it became popularly known as the "herb for green beans." In the Kujawy region, savory was grown in the garden and used as an herb in making *czarnina*, a very popular soup as well as being added to meats and marinades.

Savory was one of the nine herbs traditionally woven into a midsummer wreath.

Shepherd's Purse
Capsella bursa-pastoris
Tasnik

Considered a garden weed, shepherd's purse is a very old herbal plant in Polish folk medicine and used frequently during childbirth. A uterine bleed could be stopped by drinking 2-3 tablespoons of freshly squeezed juice from the leaves and flowers.

The use of this herb fell into decline for many years but was revived during the world wars as an effective remedy for lung hemorrhage when medicines were limited. The herbals indicate that a parasite called albugo candida often appears on shepherd's purse which also is supposed to have septic properties.

Shepherd's Purse

Silverweed
Potentilla anserina
Srebnik, gęsie ziele, drabinki

Silverweed grows throughout most of Poland on waste ground, roadsides and in pastures on damp, rich soil. One of its folk names suggests that geese are particularly fond of this plant. Even Father Kneipp seems to make notice of this in his herbal. He recommended this herb as a treatment for seizures. The afflicted individual was given hot milk three times a day to which silverweed has been cooked. In the Cracow region, silverweed was "useful for wounds, fever and stones."

Soapwort
Saponaria officinalis
Mydlnica lekarska

Marcin of Urzędow stated that, "it foams like soap." Syreniusz recalled that, "the juice from the root increases urination and is a great help to the liver. Half an ounce cooked in a glass of water removes coughs, heaviness in the chest and asthma. Used with a teaspoon of honey it purges and cleanses the womb, breaks down stones in the urine. It heals the pancreas, scabies and hard nodules."

Although soapwort grew wild, the country women often transplanted it in their gardens to have it nearby. When added to the root of burdock and nettle leaves and used for washing hair, it increased softness and added luster. Combined with the root of burdock and nettle leaves, it makes a wonderful wash, giving softness and vitality to lackluster hair. The women also used it to wash their wools and delicate fabrics.

Sorrel
Rumex acetosa
Szczaw

Sorrel is a perennial that is native to Europe and a useful Polish culinary herb. However, it was seldom grown in the garden because it was obtainable in the fields and easily resows itself. Children were encouraged to be on the lookout for nettles and sorrel when out pasturing the cattle in the spring. It was often added to the diet of those who were anemic or suffering from tuberculosis in the form of a salad or into a soup. Wild garlic could be chopped into it to make palatable.

SORREL SPRING SOUP

1 lb. sorrel leaves
2 Tbsp. butter
6 c. clear soup stock
1/2 c. sour cream
1 Tbsp. flour
Hard boiled eggs

Clean, wash and dry sorrel leaves. Chop sorrel. Sauté in butter until done (15-20 minutes) and add salt to taste. Press through sieve. Add soup stock. Mix sour cream and flour together thoroughly and combine with stock and sorrel. Let simmer 5-10 minutes. Serve with quartered eggs.

Southernwood
Artemisia abrotanum
Boże drzewko

An herb which had the power to scare away ghosts and witches, southernwood was placed in the shoe of a bride to protect her against any evil intent. Mixed with unsalted butter, southernwood helped heal wounds. A decoction of the herb was made for a woman in pain after childbirth. Cooked with honey it was given as a cough medicine.

MOTH REPELLENT

1 c. dried mint
1/2 c. dried southernwood
1/2 c. dried rosemary
2 Tbsp. powdered cloves
1 Tbsp. dried lemon peel

Mix together and place into small cloth bags.

Strawberry, Wild
Fragaria vesca
Poziomka pospolita

Wild strawberries have been in Poland since Neolithic times. They acted as food for the first Slavic tribes. The gypsies of Poland often gave wild strawberries to children who lacked an appetite or were anemic.

Marcin of Urzędow believed that the berries "eaten during heat, will cool the individual." In the herbal of Stefan Falimirz it was noted that, "wine in which wild strawberry and the seeds of parsley have been warmed, reduces kidney stones." Syreniusz also suggested its use in wine and sugar for inflammation of the lungs and pancreas, for high fever and "a bad taste in the mouth."

The root of this plant was an infallible remedy for nosebleeds when it was placed in the nose. A decoction of the leaves was applied to an area bit by spiders and the juice of the fruit and fresh leaves were used as eye drops. A tea was well known for the treatment of scurvy, gallstones, kidney stones, jaundice, colds and rashes. Fresh chopped leaves were applied to the skin that had been burned.

Fresh wild strawberry leaves were added to cooking vegetables or chicken boullion. The dried, crushed leaves were added to oat flour to make a sticky plaster for the sick. The leaves of wild strawberry mixed with the leaves of raspberry is one of the best substitutes for regular tea. A syrup was made from berries, honey and sugar.

164

Sunflower
Helianthus annuus
Słonecznik

"With flaming countenance the round sunflower
Pursues the westering sun from hour to hour."
—*Pan Tadeusz*

Oil from the seeds of sunflower was extracted for use in cooking
expecially during Lent when a strict fast was imposed. Medicinally, it
was used for pulmonary problems such as coughs and colds. The
seedcake left after the oil was removed from the seeds was also a rich
source of protein and usually fed to the livestock.

Sweet Flag
Acorus calamus
Tatarek pospolity

Botanists agree that even though calamus is widespread throughout
Poland, it was brought to Europe in the 16th century from Asia.
Growing in wet marshy regions, near rivers and streams, it was one of
the chief herbs used during Pentecost by strewing it on the floors of the
home and church. It was also a much favored herb to take to church to
be blessed on the Feast of Our Lady of the Herbs (August 15).

According to Father Kneipp, the root was dug in spring and early
summer. Dried, ground and steeped, the root was good for the treatment
of diarrhea both in humans and animals. Mixed with the leaves of hemp,
it made a salve for burns. Mixed with chamomile it rid the head of
dandruff and helped decrease hair loss.

HAIR WASH
(for dandruff and hair loss)

2 Tbsp. sweet flag
1 Tbsp. chamomile
1 qt. water

Mix calamus with the chamomile in water. Boil for 5 minutes.
Allow to cool until comfortable and wash hair.

Sycamore
Acer psuedoplatanus
Jawor

Under the shade of the sycamore a maiden waits
Her love will come along this road.
—*Polish folk song*

While growing throughout most of Europe, the sycamore is a very
prominent tree in the Carpathians mountains and is closely tied with
folklore and folk songs of the mountain people of the region. According
to the folk songs, the robbers of the region hid their booty beneath
sycamores and Janosik, the most famous robber of the Polish Tatras,
hung his cutlass on a sycamore just before he was captured and
imprisoned.

The sycamore also appeared as a symbol of love for young girls
who awaited their lover beneath a sycamore tree. In the Śląsk region,
folklore believed that women were often turned into sycamores. It was
forbidden to cut down a sycamore because if it could talk it would say,
"don't cut into me for I am a young girl."

The leaves of the sycamore had the power to remove spells and
protect against evil which is why it was used on St. John's Eve.
Decorating the windows, doors and walls of the house with the leaves
would prevent witches from entering.

Old herbals suggested that water in which the leaves of sycamore had been boiled and allowed to cool was useful in treating toothaches.

Tansy
Tanacetum vulgare
Wrotycz

A hardy, tall perennial, the button-like flowers of tansy can be found growing wild all over Europe. Professor Muszyński suggested using tansy in children who have worms. The flower of tansy was dried, ground to a powder and mixed with jam or honey. It was given to the child in the morning three days in a row.

Tansey, soaked in spirytus, was used as a liniment for treating the aches and pains of rheumatism.

Tarragon
Artemisia dracunculus
Estragon

Tarragon is a herb that came to the Poles from France (the old Polish cookbooks still carry the French name *estragonu*). It did not find as much favor in Poland as it did in France but was often used with white wine for cooking beef.

SIRLOIN WITH TARRAGON

1 lb. sirloin
2 tsp. dried tarragon
2 Tbsp. shortening

Cut sirloin into pieces. Sprinkle with tarragon and let marinate for an hour. Brown on stove in shortening, adding water as necessary. To enhance flavor, add dry white wine.

Thornapple
Datura stramonium
Dziędzierawa

Growing wild along the roads and around fences, this plant was supposedly brought to Poland from India in the 15th century by gypsies. It was used for spells and nefarious deeds by witches. All parts are poisonous.

Thistle, Carline
Carlina acaulis
Dziewięćsił, oset

Carline thistle is a hardy, clump forming perennial that bears large, stemless thistle-like flowers in summer and autumn. The flower heads are off-white or pale brown with long spiny leaves. Its favorite habitations are sunny, rocky places and poor pastures of the mountains of Europe and is plentiful in the Tatra mountains of Poland. This much loved plant has become a very popular flower motif among the mountain people of southern Poland and can be found in folk dress, wood carvings, and jewelry.

In folk life and folk medicine this plant was also valued for its ability to drive away evil. If someone's hair became inexplicably matted, it was felt to have been caused by the evil eye. One was supposed to make an infusion from the plant and rinse the hair with it to remove the mat and end the curse. It was also prescribed for impotence.

Thyme
Thymus vulgaris
Tymianek właściwy, macierzanka

Poland can thank Queen Bona Sforza for bringing thyme from her native Italy and having it grown in monastery gardens. It was at one time an amulet offered to knights in tournaments and used to wash their wounds. It was also used in a mixture with rosemary to heal eczema and calm a cough. Collected on St. John's Eve, an infusion of it aided women in childbirth. Older women bathed in it, believing that it made them appear younger. They also used it to make poultices for rheumatic pains in the arms. Young infants and children refusing to thrive were bathed in it.

THYME BATH
(to strengthen and decrease pains)

2 c. dried thyme
5 qts. water

Boil the thyme in the water for a few minutes in a covered pot under medium flame. Strain. Add to 38 C. bath water. The bath should not last longer than 15 minutes.

THYME DRINK
(for children)

1 Tbsp. thyme
1 Tbsp. anise
1 Tbsp. primrose

Make a mixture of the thyme, anise and primrose. Add 1 Tbsp. of the herb mixture to one cup of boiling water. Give 1 Tbsp. every 2 hours. It can be sweetened with honey.

Valerian
Valeriana officinalis
Walerian

Valerian grows wild in moist, damp places throughout Poland. The root, dug up in the fall or early spring, was used a great deal for treatment of nervous conditions.

Vervain
Verbena officinalis
Koszyczki Najswiętszej Marii Panny

One of the much loved herbs dedicated to the Blessed Virgin, vervain was often taken to church to be blessed on the Feast of Our Lady of the Herbs.

Polish women believed it helpful in matters of the heart, but it was chiefly used as a tea or tonic to promote easier childbirth.

Violet
Viola adorata.
Fiołek

A decoction from violets is injested like a tea for whooping cough. For a cold, gather the leaves of violet with the dew still on them; boil and drink.

Father Kneipp recommended the flowers and leaves of violet for teas, especially for severe coughs and strong headaches.

VIOLET TEA

1/4 c. dried violet leaves
2 1/2 c. boiling water

Pour the boiling water over the dried leaves. Steep and then strain. Adults may drink a glass two to three times a day; children may take two to three tablespoons a day.

Wallpepper, Stone Crop
Sedum acre
Rozchodnik

As a treatment for a sore throat, wallpepper was scalded and applied to the throat. The juice from the leaves, crushed and applied to cancerous ulcers as a poultice, brought relief and healing if changed frequently. Rinsing the mouth with a decoction of the herb strengthened the gums and decreased the damage caused by scurvy. Fried with an equal amount of thyme in unsalted fat, it made a salve for wounds.

Walnut
Juglans regia
Orzech włoski

The walnut tree was brought to the Opole and Pomerania regions of Poland in the 12th and 13th century. A decoction of the leaf was rubbed on cattle to decrease bites by flies and gadflies. A tincture made of the young, green nuts was a universal treatment for all types of diarrhea. A decoction of the leaves was made with sugar to treat rickets as well as remedy internal hemorrhage, gout and parasites. A chronic cough was relieved by drinking an infusion of the leaves. Wounds and ulcerated skin were treated with a liniment made from the oil-steeped leaves.

SALVE
(for pimples and trauma areas)

1 Tbsp. chopped fresh walnut leaves
1 c. sunflower oil

Place the chopped fresh walnut leaves in the sunflower oil and allow to stand for a week. Then heat in double boiler for three hours. Strain through gauze, cook another half hour and add a tablespoon of wax to thicken.

Wheat
Triticum vulgare
Pszenica

"..the wheat stood upright boldly, as straight as so many pillars, lifting their glossy and dusky heads."
—*The Peasants: Spring*

Wheat was one of Poland's main food staples. The bran from the kernals of wheat, scalded with chamomile and vinegar, was applied to the side of the face when teeth hurt.

Willow, White
Salix alba
Wierzba biała

In folk medicine, the bark of willow was used for fevers and coughs, for treating rheumatism, headaches and also diarrhea. A tea made of the leaves was supposed to help pains in the chest. Externally, it was used for wounds that refused to heal. It was blessed traditionally on Palm Sunday and also used to bless the cattle when sent out to pasture for the first time in the spring. Swallowing pussy willow buds assured health and prosperity for the entire year.

Young branches were used to make baskets and weave wattle

fences. Its soft wood was converted into various household goods. The bark was used to make a dye to color wool and silk a cinnamon or yellow, depending on the mordant (either lye or alum). A decoction of the root can dye red, if boiled long enough.

WILLOW
(for wounds filled with pus)

1 Tbsp. willow bark
1 c. water

Add the dry and crumbled bark to the water and boil 10 minutes. Strain and drink one half glass 2 to 3 times a day or apply directly to wound.

Wormwood
Artemisia absinthium
Piołun

Wormwood appears all over Poland in wasteland and roadsides as well as established gardens. Aromatic and bitter to the taste, the chief part of the plant used for healing was the leaves. The old herbals advised that once the pungent odor wore off, the leaves had to be replaced to continue being effective. Syreniusz advised that wormwood "warms a cold stomach, and awakens the appetite." An infusion of the herb was a treatment for stomach complaints and disorders. A mixture of fresh chopped leaves and one egg white was applied to injured areas. A decoction of the leaves was used as a compress for burning eyes. In Russia it was used to heal wounds and cleanse the blood—especially wormwood picked in May.

In the Middle Ages in Poland, it was added to ink in order to protect books against the ravages of mice and insects. It was also sprinkled on linens to drive away bugs. In some parts of Poland fresh wormwood was used to keep fleas away from the bed by placing fresh leaves beneath the sheets and sprinkling them around the bed. To shoo away flies in barns and byres, bouquets of wormwood were hung in front of the door. To exterminate fleas from dogs, bathe in a concentrated solution of wormwood. Bees avoid areas where wormwood grows.

WORMWOOD INFUSION
(for stomach troubles)

1/2 tsp. wormwood
1 c. boiling water

Pour the boiling water over the wormwood in a covered teapot. Steep for 15 minutes. Drink 1 Tbsp. of the hot drink before meals.

WORMWOOD INFUSION
(as an aid to digestion)

1/2 tsp. wormwood
1 c. boiling water

Pour the boiling water over the wormwood in a covered teapot. Steep for 15 minutes. Add 15 to 20 drops of the infusion to a whiskey glass full of vodka.

WORMWOOD MOUTH RINSE
(for bad breath)

1/2 tsp. wormwood
1 c. boiling water

Pour the boiling water over the wormwood in a covered teapot. Steep for 15 minutes. Add one half of a tablespoon of the infusion to one third cup of water. Brush teeth with this solution.

HERBS AND FLOWERS

Yarrow
Achillea millefolium
Krawnik pospolity

In the Middle Ages, yarrow was grown in Poland in the garden monasteries of the Dominicans and Benedictines.

Marcin of Urzędow suggested poultices of yarrow for inflammed and pus filled wounds. Syreniusz suggested its use for internal bleeding, diarrhea and pain in the intestines. He suggested that the herb is good boiled in wine and taken for "colic and biting in the stomach. Mashed and applied to the body it will stop nosebleeds and decrease tooth pain if the root is chewed."

Country women rubbed the fresh leaves in their hands and applied it to bleeding areas to stop the flow of blood. The juice squeezed from the fresh leaves was applied to open sores and fresh wounds. Boiled in white wine it was considered a medication for vaginal discharge. A salve was made for wounds, ulcers and fistulas. The powdered dry leaf was smoked like tobacco to cure headaches. In the 18th century, extracts and oils made from yarrow were sold in apothecary shops across Poland.

The finely chopped leaves made a good addition to the regular feed of poultry, especially young turkeys.

It is also one of the herbs blessed on August 15 on the Feast of Our Lady of the Herbs.

Yew, English
Taxus baccata
Cis

This tree is found throughout Poland, with many villages named after the tree where it is found locally.

During the time of the Piasts, the yew was already famous as a hardwood and used in building homes. It also appears in folk songs often, referring to gates, chests and especially tables. For instance, on a table made of yew, a young maiden spills rue to make a wreath for her wedding day.

Medicinally, the most frequently cited use of yew was in treating rabies. The bitten area was washed and tiny shavings of the bark were applied.

CHAPTER V

Growing Your Polish Herb and Flower Garden

Whether you live on a country estate or in a city apartment, you can have a garden. And whether it's an in-the-ground garden or just a few pots on the windowsill, there is something very comforting and satisfying in planting an herb or a flower with which you can identify and be attached to through a sense of history and tradition. To know that a particular plant was a favorite among cottage gardeners or to recreate a knot garden pattern that was in existence in Poland almost three hundred years ago, can fulfill a need to be connected with one's heritage. Even the smallest garden with ties to the past can be a source of comfort, satisfaction and a great deal of pride.

To these ends, I have made some suggestions in the next few pages. Although it is impossible to adequately cover the scope of soil requirements, gardening zones and landscaping problems in a way that would meet your special needs, the really good news is that there are many wonderful gardening books and magazines on the market that will help fullfill your every gardening desire. If you've never tried your hand at a garden or even a flower box, but would like to do so now, start with a visit to your local public library or favorite bookstore and read about gardening in your area. People who love to garden also love to share their knowledge and there are lots of wonderful books out there to both answer your questions and inspire you.

When you feel you've read enough, visit herb gardens and nurseries with display gardens to check plants for size, color and shape. Spend some time looking over what you'd like and then make a list of plants that strike your fancy. Take the winter months to decide what kind of garden you want—culinary garden, mixture of perennial flowers and herbs, a knot garden, an herbal tea garden, an alpine garden. If you enjoy cooking a great deal, you may wish to focus on Polish cooking and plant a culinary herb garden that will be useful in your cuisine. If you are a craft person you may wish to plant a garden for dyeing. Or, if the healing properties of plants intrigue you, you can base your garden on folk medicine with comfrey and wormwood at its heart. If you haven't already done so, talk to your Polish relatives and ask them about their gardens, what plants they are partial to and why. Can a grandparent remember what flowers were grown in her parents garden in Poland? What herbs were used when she was sick? What flowers did she take to church?

Sometimes we think that if our parents or grandparents had such information, they would offer it as a matter of course, however, this is not always so. My own mother, an avid gardener and user of folk medicine, never talked much about what she did until I began to ask her questions. She then recalled that her mother had had a white lilac bush growing near the gate in front of the house and that there were irises, too, pale white and white and yellow lilies. Such small memories can often become the basis for a very special garden.

Before you reach for a spade, take a stroll through your yard to determine where you would like to plant your garden. Perhaps you'd like a traditional, informal cottage garden in the front of your home. If that's not suitable, plant it near the back door or at a place that suits your purpose. Maybe you would like to recreate one of the formal knot gardens. Or perhaps you already have an existing vegetable garden, and you may just want to set aside a little bit of room for the culinary or medicinal herbs that have peaked your interest.

Herbs are hardy, easy to grow and will flourish just about anywhere if a few simple needs are met. Most herbs need full sun or partial sun, so look for a spot that receives at least four to six hours of sunlight a day. They also require soil that is well drained: check your soil. Soil is critical to the success of a garden and healthy herbs require good drainage and decent soil. Ideally, they prefer a light open soil which is well areated yet able to retain moisture and nutrients. Some soils are very sandy, allowing water to flow through an area before any plants in the vicinity can take advantage of it. The addition of compost will also help absorb and hold water, making it available to plants. Soil that is full of clay is also problematic as it doesn't allow water to drain off and ends up drowning the roots. The answer for both problems is the addition of compost or spahgnum moss. Compost is decomposed organic matter. The addition of organic matter to clay that has been loosened will make water and nutrients available for any herb or flower. It can be made from grass clippings, leaves, garden weeds, sawdust, leafy kitchen scraps, woodshavings and wood ashes. Manure from horses, cows, rabbits or poultry is available at special rates to a gardener. It is important to remember not to apply fresh manure directly to a garden containing new plants. The high nitrogen content can damage the plants. It is best to pile it up and let it rot for a few months before adding it to your garden.

Herbs prefer a neutral or slighly alkaline soil with a pH of 6 to 7 1/2. Simple testing kits are available at garden centers or you can send a soil sample to your local Cooperative Extension service, a section of the U.S. Department of Agriculture that gives assistance to farmers and gardeners. Soil that is acidic could use lime scattered over the surface or wood ashes from the fireplace or woodburning stove.

Start your garden from seeds, established plants or from cuttings. Established plants give results more quickly than seeds, but growing from seed can be another enlightening, exhilarating and/or frustrating experience, so make your own decision. For skilled and unskilled gardeners alike, you learn what is best for you and what will work in your garden by trial and error. While there is no getting away from the fact that gardening is work, it's a pleasurable kind of work with fun and interesting offshoots: make drawings of what you've planted; keep a diary or journal of plants doing well or lost to rabbits and mix in your gardening thoughts; take photographs of your mother's and grandmother's gardens, as well as your own; start a garden club. Make gardening what you want it to be.

Knot Garden

The Oxford English Dictionary defines knot gardens as a flower bed laid-out in an intricate design. The pattern for a knot garden can be just about anything—entwined initials, a family emblem, coat of arms or motto. It can also be gratifying to plant a knot garden in a design from the past, such as the one depicted in the earlier pages of this book.

The design for a knot garden was almost always designed in a square and made of low hedges such as boxwood (commonly just called box in gardening circles), germander, santolina or dwarf lavender. Box and santolina are good choices from which to create the design because they are evergreen and can be clipped and kept looking neat. Box, particularly dwarf box, is very hardy, and can be clipped very close to the ground. Plant first whatever shrub or perennial you've chosen to create the hedge. Then fill the inside of the hedges with herbs and flowers. For instance, you can fill the inside of a knot garden with violets, primroses, lilies or minature roses. Or, plant a variety of medicinal herbs such as hyssop and chamomile or some culinary herbs of your choice. Sometimes white stones, pebbles or colored sand were placed within the hedges for color too, depending on the desired effect or preferences of the gardener.

When you decide to put in a knot garden, first work out the design on paper. Mark it on the ground using string and sticks. Remember that knot gardens show well from a high elevation, such as the upper floors of a large house or on the lower slope of a property where the design can be viewed from above. Care must be taken, however, to make sure the area is not prone to wetness or frost pockets or it can be disastrous for the plants.

Windowsill and Patio Gardening

You don't need an outdoor herb garden to enjoy a herbal harvest or the lovely blossoms of a flower. Many herbs and flowers are just as happy growing in a pot. This is ideal for herbalists in the wintertime but especially important for those with limited space such as city-dwellers or condominium owners. For them, the windowsill, a small patio, a fire escape, rooftop, windowbox or an outside window ledge are all possibilities for enjoying the tastes and scents of herbs and flowers.

For growing individual herbs, pots are the most practical and useful. Plastic pots are both lightweight and easy to clean and store. However, if you are a traditionalist, stick to clay or terra cotta pots which are porous. Unglazed clay pots are very traditional, and, for my money, I feel they have the greater aesthetic appeal. They also allow water to evaporate through the clay.

New clay pots should be soaked in water for 24 hours before use. Old and used pots should be clean of any previous plant soil and mineral deposits. The pot should have adequate drainage (at least one hole) at the bottom of the pot. Layer the bottom with broken crockery or pebbles to aid drainage. A good potting soil from a garden center should be used to plant the herb. Most herbs need four to six hours of sunlight but some, like parsley, thyme and mint can survive with a little less. Without the earth's nutrients to draw on, potted herbs must be fed regulary. A diluted organic fertilizer should be given once a month.

A word about geraniums. The geranium is one annual that can give you more mileage by being brought indoors when cold winds begin to blow. Most books will not recommend digging your geraniums out of the garden or window box to pot them up inside the house. Plants dug from the garden can become riddled with insects from the soil. However, I must admit that I do just that. And yes, the plants do lose their leaves and look positively awful for a little while after bringing them in, but eventually they stabilize and come March, give forth a show of pink and red flowers. I do this because it's the way my mother always treated her geraniums—year in, year out. One of my fondest childhood memories is being sent to the pantry for a jar of canned beets or peaches and finding the geraniums flowering on the windowsill, tilted towards the sunny window, watching the wintery landscape outside. When my mother came to live with me, she also brought her geraniums. Now, every fall, along with my mother's help, I dig up the geraniums we've planted in the spring, pot them up again in the fall and place them on my kitchen window expectantly waiting for the winter day when they'll bloom again.

Occasionally, I do resort to the recommended way of bringing geraniums inside. The experts suggest taking root cuttings that you clip in midsummer. I do this because the original geraniums have become big and unwieldy and I want to continue growing geraniums from those that originally grew on the pantry window of my childhood home.

The best way to take root cuttings is to cut about four inches of stem just below a leaf axil. Remove the lower leaves and dip the sliced end of the cutting into a commercial rooting powder. Insert the cutting into a perlite and peat mixture or coarse sand. After the cuttings are in the rooting medium, water well and place the container in a tightly closed plastic bag. Set in indirect light and after approximately ten days check for rooting by gently pulling on the cutting. If there is resistance, the cutting is rooted. Transplant to a larger pot, using rich porous soil. Move to a window and water whenever the surface soil becomes dry.

Collecting Herbs

As a rule, the flavor and medicinal properties of an herb are at their peak immediately prior to flowering. This is the time when the active components of the plant are of the best quality. Herbs should be collected in the morning before the heat of the day has dissipated the plant's essential oils.

If you are seeking the flowering tops of a plant, collect them as the flowers are beginning to open. Avoid the overblown or fading flower. Use a good knife, scissors or gardening shears in order to make a clean cut and prevent bruising.

Collect seeds when they are almost ripe, before they fall to the ground.

When harvesting the root of the plant, be sure to gather in the autumn, at the end of the growing season, when the root is mature and storing as much food as possible. The root may be collected in any weather, at any time of day. The leaves, however, should be gathered in the morning, before the heat of the day has begun but after the morning dew has dried.

Long-stemmed herbs like mint, yarrow and southernwood should be gathered in small bunches, tied together at the ends and hung upside-down in a dim, dry and airy place. Most herbs will dry quite successfully if handled this way. Wash first, then pat dry carefully and cover with a paper bag to protect from dust and insects. Attics, a warm garden shed or a darkened spare room are suitable places for drying herbs. Do not place them near a stove or sink; steam interferes with drying. Furthermore, avoid drying herbs against a wall. This blocks out circulation and delays or interferes with the drying process. Drying racks can still be purchased at antique shops, flea markets and garage sales. An old-fashioned window screen that has been cleaned can serve as a drying rack, especially for whole flowerheads or individual leaves and petals, as from roses or scented geraniums. Stacked one on top of the other in layers with bricks at the corners to keep the herbs from touching and the air circulating works effectively. Drying trays can also be made with screening and 2-by-2 lumber. An open weave basket will also work effectively if scattered in a single layer on the bottom. The herbs can also be dried by placing them on a cookie sheet in a warm oven with the door left ajar. The oven method was traditionally used by Polish housewives. After removing baked bread from the oven, the housewife placed her herbs inside to dry. The herbs dried quickly, preserving their flavor and aroma. When dry, they were crumbled and placed into cloth bags or bottles with corks.

The herbs will take from 2 to 10 days to dry, depending on the humidity. In humid weather, the process may take longer. Dry herbs should be brittle to the touch and crumble easily. It is important to remember to store the herbs immediately. Strip the leaves carefully from the stems and store them tightly in airtight containers such as wooden boxes, or dark glass bottles that will keep out light and moisture. Label each bottle with the name of the herb and the date.

Herb Vinegars

A bottle of herb vinegar will allow you to enjoy the taste of your favorite herb in the kitchen long after the garden has gone to sleep in the winter. My personal favorite is dill vinegar, which I use in cold summer soups and tomato and cucumber salads, as well as added flavoring to potato salads.

Pick the herbs as previously recommended. Slightly bruise them and loosely fill a clean jar or bottle. Using white cider or wine vinegar as the base, heat the vinegar. Pour on warmed, but not hot, vinegar to fill the jar and cap with an acid-proof lid. Clear wine bottle and corks are especially useful, as are gallon glass jugs if your making in quantity to give as gifts, or the old-fashioned canning jars with the glass lids. Set in a sunny window to help release the oils. Shake occasionally and test for flavor. If a stronger flavor is required, strain the vinegar through a cheesecloth and repeat with fresh herbs. Or, if the herb vinegar is to your taste, either store as is or strain out the old herbs and rebottle with a fresh sprig of the herb for accurate identification and visual appeal. Use in any recipe that calls for vinegar.

Herb Butters and Cheeses

Soften a quarter pound of butter. Chop a few fresh sprigs of your favorite herb, about one tablespoon—parsley, dill, chives, tarragon or caraway seeds and add to the softened butter. Add a tablespoon of lemon for extra zip especially when baking or broiling fish. Mix together until smooth. Chill briefly before serving or using to allow flavors to blend.

The same method can be used for adding herbs to soft cheeses such as cream cheese or farmers cheese.

Creating an Herb Wreath

Making wreaths from grains (oats, wheat and rye) as well as flowers and herbs is a rich part of Polish tradition. To make your wreath, gather together the herbs and flowers you would like in your arrangement. Thyme, lavender, mint and sage as well as roses, yarrow, feverfew and smaller branches of trees and shrubs can easily be worked into a wreath. While everything could be dried and used later, it is easier and more traditional to make the wreath while the stems are still fresh and supple.

If possible, work the wreath in the old-fashioned manner of braiding together some vines or long grasses into a circle to act as the base or using a supple willow twig tied firmly together in a circle as a frame. Attach herbs and flowers firmly to the base with thin wire, string or by tucking into the base. Overlap herbs and flowers so that the base is completely covered and stems of the previous bunch do not show. Add twigs, dried seed pods or nuts to flesh out the wreath or fill in gaps if necessary.

Leave the wreath to dry in a dark, well ventilated place. Hang on doors or walls.

Glossary of Terms

Aphrodisiac—a substance which stimulates sexual excitement and sometimes ability

Bronchus—one of the main branches of the trachea

Compote—a dish of fruits cooked in syrup

Compress—a piece of linen or cloth soaked in an herbal infusion or decoction and applied externally

Consumption—older name for wasting away of the body; tuberculosis of the lungs

Decoction—a herbal dose obtained by boiling or simmering roots, barks twigs and berries. Place the herb in a saucepan, preferably enamel or stainless steel and add cold water. Bring to a boil and let simmer sometimes up to an hour until volume of water has been reduced by one-third. Strain and store. Only enough should be made for one day's use at a time to assure freshness

Distillation—the process of heating a liquid to convert it to vapor, condensing the vapor and collecting the condensation

Diuretic—a substance that promotes the flow of urine

Dropsy—an older term for swelling of the body or body parts

Dysentery—inflammation of the intestine, characterized by diarrhea containing mucus and blood, causing pain to evacuate the bowels

Eczema—an acute or chronic inflammation of the skin

Expectorant—a substance that encourages phlegm to be coughed up from the lungs

Furuncle (boil)—an abcess of the subcutaneous layers of the skin

Infusion—a herbal dose made in much the same way as tea and is used for flowers and leafy parts of plants. Put the herb in a pot with a tight fitting lid. Always use enamel, stainless steel or earthenware pans or teapots. Pour in boiling water. Leave to steep for 10 minutes then pour through a nylon sieve or strainer into a teacup. Store the rest in a cool place. It should be made fresh each day for three doses

Jaundice—a condition characterized by yellowness of the skin, caused by excessive amounts of bilirubin in the blood

Lactation—the secretion of milk

Maceration—the extraction of a drug from a plant by steeping it in a solvent

Phlegm—thick, elastic mucous secreted by the cells lining the air passages

Poultice—warm or hot application of crushed herbs or extracts of a plant and applied to bruised or inflammed skin

Purgative—a strong laxative; any substance that causes evacuation of the bowel

Salve—a soothing ointment

Scrofula—tuberculosis of the lymphatic glands, especially of the neck

Scurvy—a nutritional disorder caused by lack of vitamin C

Spirytus—Polish equivalent to 95% proof alcohol

Syrup—made from honey or refined sugar and may be used to preserve infusions and decoctions. Add honey or sugar to a heated decoction or infusion in a saucepan. Stir until dissolved. Allow the mixture to cool and pour into a clean bottle that will take a cork. Seal with the cork

Tincture—a solution of extracts of medicinal plants obtained by steeping the dried or fresh herbs in alcohol. The alcohol acts as a preservative and tinctures will keep for at least two years. Put the herb into a large jar and cover with vodka/water mixture. Seal the jar and store in a cool place for a couple of weeks, shaking occasionally

Sources for Gardeners

The Antique Rose Emporium
Route 5 Box 143
Brenham, TX 77833
1-800-441-0002

Hundreds of roses to choose from including old-fashioned varieties, books and videos on growing roses, rustic cedar furniture for old fashioned gardens. Informational catalog with color photographs: $5.00.

Brittingham Plant Farms
P.O. Box 2538 Dept. HFP5
Salisbury, MD 21802
(410)749-5153

Specializes in raspberries, blueberries, rhubarb and blackberries. Free catalog.

Brown's Edgewood Gardens
2611 Corrine Drive
Orlando, FL 32803
(407)896-3203

Wide selection of potted medicinal and culinary herbs, herbal teas and garden markers.

Carroll Gardens
444 E. Main Street
P.O. Box 310
Westminister, MD 21158
(410)848-5422

POLISH HERBS, FLOWERS & FOLK MEDICINE

Extremely broad selection of herbs, perennials, roses, trees and shrubs. The $3.00 catalog will bring everything to your doorstep for starting a garden.

Country Gardens
Route 1 Box 549
Toms Brook, VA 22660
(703)436-3746

Herbs, perennials and dried flowers.

Country Road Herb Farm and Gift Barn
1497 Pymatuning Lake Road
Andover, OH 44003
(216)577-1932

Largest distributor of medicinal and culinary herbs in northeast Ohio. Books. Teas. Catalog: $2.00.

Dreams End Farm
8655 S. Feddick Road
Hamburg, NY 14075-7007
(716)942-3330

Display gardens with plants for sale at the farm. Herbal items, potpourri, books by mail. Offers workshops.

Forest Farm
990 Tethrow Road
Williams, OR 97544-9599
(503)846-7269

SOURCES FOR GARDENERS

Bee plants, roses, hops, solomon's seal as well as numerous shrubs and trees including elderberry and boxwood. Catalog: $3.00.

Forks of the Grand Herb Company
32 Golf Links Road
Paris, Ontario, Canada N3L 1R3
(519)442-2992

Herbs, straw and vine bee-skeps. Gift shop and display gardens.

Freshops
36180 Kings Valley Hwy
Philomath, OR 97370
(503)929-2763

Specializes in selling female hop rhizomes as well as dried hops. Catalog: $1.00.

Frey's Dahlias
12054 Brick Road
Turner, OR 97392
(503)743-3910

All style of dahlia blooms.

Greenmantle Nursery
3010 Ettersburg Rd.
Garberville, CA 95442
(707)986-7504

Old garden roses, apples, pears and plums. Catalog: $3.00.

Greenfield Herb Garden
P.O. Box 9
Depot and Harrison
Shipshewanna, IN 46595
(219)768-7110

Great selection of herb seeds including sorrel and nasturtium. Bee-skeps, fragrance oils and essential oils. Many herb books on a wide array of topics. Catalog: $1.50.

The Herb Garden
P.O. Box 773
Pilot Mountain, N.C. 27041
(910)368-2723

Good selection of artemesias, lavender, thyme and mint plants. Dried herbs and teas, books. Catalog: $4.00.

Hortico, Inc.
723 Robson Road RR#1
Waterdown, Ontario, Canada L0R 2H1
(416)689-6984

Wide variety of perennials, trees and shrubs. Rose, shrub or perennial list: $3.00 each.

Historical Roses
1657 West Jackson Street
Painesville, OH 44077
(216)357-7270

Old garden roses including Rosa gallica officinalis and Rosa centifolia, climbing roses and hybrid teas.

Heritage Rose Gardens
16831 Mitchell Creek Drive
Fort Bragg, CA 95437
(707)964-3748

Organically grown roses. Carry gallica and centifolia roses, old fashioned ramblers and climbers as well as hardy rugosa roses. Catalog: $1.50.

Heirloom Old Garden Roses
24062 Riverside Drive N.E.
St. Paul, OR 97137
(503)538-1576

Numerous old fashioned garden roses.

Kurt Bluemel, Inc.
2740 Greene Lane
Baldwin, MD 21013-9523
(410)557-9785

Carries sweet flag (calamus), poppy, peony, geraniums and a host of other perennial plants, grasses and ferns. Catalog: $3.00.

Milaegers Gardens
4838 Douglas Avenue
Racine, WN 53402-2498
(414)639-2371

Very wide selection of perennials including old-fashioned single hollyhocks, aconite and foxglove.

Northwind Nursery and Orchards
7910 335th Ave. NW
Princeton, MN 55371
(612) 389-4920

Hardy, organically grown apple, pear and plum trees as well as wine grapes and raspberries.

Pickering Nursuries, Inc.
670 Kingston Road
Pickering, Ontario, Canada L1V 1A6

Extensive assortment (700+) of roses. Color catalog: $3.00

Staneks Garden Center
2929 East 27th Avenue
Spokane, WA 99223
(509)535-2939

Wide selection of roses, raspberries and nut trees. Free catalog.

The Thyme Garden
20546 Alsea Hwy.
Alsea, OR 97324
(503)487-8671

Common to exotic herbs. Hops, marjorams, rue and of course, numerous varieties of thyme. Display gardens. Catalog:$2.00, refundable with first order.

Triple Oaks Nursery and Florist
Delsea Drive
Franklinville, NJ 08322
(609)694-4274

Polish owned and operated. Offers all the traditional Polish herbs including marjoram, sorrel, zubrowka grass as well as myrtle plants, pussy willow bushes and more. Books, recipes and gift items.

Well Sweep Herb Farm
317 Mt. Bethel Road
Port Murray, NJ 07865
(908)852-5390

Wide selection of herbs and perennials including St. John's wort. Free catalog.

White Flower Farm
P.O. Box 50 Route 63
Litchfield, CT 06759-0050
(203)496-9600

Wide array of herbs, old fashioned perennials and shrubs as well as gardening tools and suppplies. Display gardens.

Miscellaneous

Brookside Studio
Rt.1 Box 100
Otto Maples Road
Little Valley, NY 14755

Offers award winning limited edition prints from Rural Heritage Collection Series of country scenes, cows and hollyhocks. Catalog: $2.00.

Craft World Tours
6776 Warboys Road
Byron, NY 14422
(716)548-2667

Offers folk art tours to Poland including skansens (museum villages), historical old city centers, castles and cathedrals.

Herb Companion
201 East Fourth St.
Loveland, CO 80537
(303) 669-7672

Magazine devoted to all aspects of herbs including history, recipes, herb shops and gardens open to the public.

Hogshed Studio
8420 Otto Maples Road
Little Valley, NY 14755
(716) 257-9549

Beautiful stoneware bird feeders. Polish herb markers.

Bibliography

Bowe, Patrick. *Gardens in Central Europe*. New York: M.T. Train/Scala Books, 1991.

Bystron, Jan Stanisław. *Dzieje Obyczajów w Dawnej Polsce. Tom I.* [History of the Customs of Old Poland. Volume I]. Warszawa: Państwowy Instytut Wydawniczy, 1976.

Chętnik, Adam. "Jałowiec w życiu, Obrzędach i Wierzenie Kurpiów," [Juniper in the Life, Customs and Beliefs of the Kurpie People], *Ziemia*, 1928, p.269-274.

Chmielińska, Anna. "O Ziołach Leczniczych i Ich Stosowanie w Łowickiem," [Of Healing Herbs and Their Use in Łowicz], *Ziemia*, 1933, p.98-101.

Ciołek, Gerard. *Ogrody Polskie* [Polish Gardens]. Warszawa: Arkady, 1978.

Ciołek, Gerard. *Zarys Historii Kompozycji Ogrodowej w Polsce.* [Outline of the Historical Composition of Gardens in Poland]. Łódź: Panstwowe Wydawnictwo Naukowe, 1955.

Dmochowski, Zbigniew. *The Architecture of Poland*. London: Polish Research Center, 1956.

Fischer, Adam. "Drzewa w Wierzeniach i Obrzędach Ludu Polskiego," [Trees in Beliefs and Customs of Polish People], *Lud*, 1937, p.60-75.

Fischer, Adam. "Klon i Jawor w Kulturze Ludu Polskiego," [The Maple and Sycamore in Polish Folk Culture], *Ziemia*, 1932, p.124-126.

Gloger, Zygmunt. *Encyklopedia Staropolska Tom III-IV.* [Encyclopedia of Old Poland, Volumes III and IV]. Warszawa: Wiedza Powszechna, 1985.

Gumowska, Irena. *Ziółka i my.* [Herbs and Us]. Warszawa: Wydawnictwo PTTK "Kraj," 1983.

Hellwig, Zygmunt. *Byliny w parku i ogrodzie.* [Perennials in the Park and Garden]. Warszawa: Panstwowe Wydawnictwo Rolnicze i Leśne, 1975.

POLISH HERBS, FLOWERS & FOLK MEDICINE

Hensla, W. and Pazdura, J. eds. *Historia Kultura Materialna, Tom I-V* [History of the Material Culture Volumes I]. Wrocław: Zakład Narodowy Imienia Ossolińskich Wydawnictwo Polskiej Akademii Nauk, 1981.

Karwowski, S. "Choroby i Medycyna na Sląsku," [Illness and Medicine in Silesia], *Lud*, 1896, p.289-292.

Kniepp, Ks. *Zielnik czli Atlas Roślin Leczniczych*. [Herbal or An Atlas of Healing Plants]. Bawarja: Nakład Księgarni J. Kösla, 1892.

Kosiński, Władysław. "Zapiski Etnologiczne," [Ethnological Notes], *Wisła*, 1890, p.867.

Kostrzewski, Józef. Kultura Prapolska. [Primitive Polish Culture]. Poznan: Instytut Zachodni, 1949.

Kuźnicka, B. et.al., *Zioła i ich Stosowanie*. [Herbs and Their Preparation]. Warszawa: Państwowy Zakład Wydawnictw Lekarskich, 1984.

Majdecki, Longin. *Historia Ogrodów*. [History of Gardens]. Warszawa: Państwowy Wydawnictwo Naukowe, 1981.

Muszyński, Jan. *Roslinne Leki Ludowe*. [Healing Plants of the People]. Warszawa: Ludowa Społdzielnia Wydawnicza, 1958.

Muszyński, Jan. *Ziołolecznictwo i Leki Roślinne* [Herbology and Healing Plants]. Łódź: 1946.

Seweryn,T., Szewczyck, Z., and Woleńska, M., *Kultura Materialna*. [Materialna Folk Culture]. Kraków: 1954.

Siarkowski, Wł. Ks. " Lecznictwo Ludowe," [Folk Healing], *Wisła*, 1891, p. 903-904.

Staniszewski, Zofia. "Lecznictwo Ludowe," [Folk Healing], *Wisła*, 1895, p.122-126.

Sulisz, Józef. "Zapiski Etnograficzne z Ropczyc," [Ethnographic Notes from Ropczyc], *Lud*, 1906, p.57-63.

Świątkowski, Henryk. *Łowickie Budownictwo Ludowe*. [Architecture of the People of Łowicz]. Warszawa: Muzeum Narodowe w Warszawie, 1973.

BIBLIOGRAPHY

Szafer, W. *Concise History of Botany in Cracow Against the Background of Six Centuries of the Jagellonian University.* Translated from the Polish. Published for Smithsonian Institution and National Science Foundation. Warsaw: 1969.

Szafer, W. *Rośliny Polskie.* [Plants of Poland]. Warszawa: Panstwowe Wydawnictwo Naukowe, 1976.

Szulczewski, W. "Rośliny w Mianownictwie, Prezesądach i Lecznictwie Ludu Wielkopolskiego," [Plants in Nomenclature, Superstition and Healing of the People of Greater Poland], *Lud*, 1932, p.93-100.

Turowska, Irena and Olesiński, Aleksander. *Zarys Zielarstwa.* [An Outline of the Study of Herbs]. Warszawa: Państwowy Zakład Wydawnictw Lekarskich, 1951.

Tyklowa, Danuta. "Lecznictwo Ludowe," [Folk Healing], *Etnografia Polska*, t.XXXVIII, 1984, p.201-222.

Tyszyńska-Kownacka, D. and Stanek, T. *Zioła w Polskim Domu.* [Herbs in a Polish Home]. Warszawa: Wydawnictwo Watra, 1991.

Udziela, Marjan. *Medycyna i Przesądy Lecznicze Ludu Polskiego.* [Medicine and Superstitous Healing of the Polish People]. Warszawa: Skład Główny w Księgarni M. Arcta, 1891.

Wawrzeniecki, Marjan. "Nieco o Roślinach, z których Wite są Wianki, Święcone na Boże Ciało," [A Little on Plants Which Are Woven into Wreaths and Blessed on Corpus Christi], *Wisła*, 1916-17, p.19-23.

Weryho Władysław. "Z Medycyny Ludowej" [From Folk Medcine], *Wisła*, 1888, p.604-607.

Wiśniewski, A. "Lecznictwo Ludowe zebrane w Sokołowie pod Rzeszowem," [Folk Medicine in Sokołów near Rzeszów], *Wisła*, 1891, p.640-645.

Index

INDEX

INDEX

203

INDEX

Index of Scientific Names

INDEX